85 Best Canadian Stories

Edited by David Helwig & Sandra Martin

Fifteen years ago, the first of the Oberon short-story anthologies appeared; one of the contributors was Marian Engel. As this fifteenth book goes to press, news has come of her premature death, at 51, of cancer.

In 1970, when I phoned Marian Engel to ask if she might have something for a new Oberon project, we had never met; she was a young novelist whose second book, *The Honeyman Festival,* had just appeared with a young press, the House of Anansi. I met her at the first gathering of the Writers' Union a year or so later—in those days (impossible not to regret) when the Union seemed like a fiction writer's club—and over the years, we ran into each other at meetings, on trains, in subway stations. She was someone I was always pleased to see, and I felt the same way about her fiction. The books were like Marian Engel herself in their combination of humanity and intelligence.

It was characteristic of Marian that she could talk about personal matters, her parents, her children, without ever seeming indiscreet. Her openness had its own kind of tact. When, for a short while, she wrote a column for the Toronto *Star,* she wrote essays on prostitution and abortion that were models of concern, decency and generosity. Even a letter of support she wrote for a writer applying to the Canada Council for a grant sticks in my mind for its directness, its liveliness. She was one of those writers who put on paper not just what she thought and imagined, but what she was.

For some years before her death, Marian Engel knew that she had cancer, "One of the controllable cancers," as she once described it, and while she talked of a new novel, she probably sensed that she didn't have the strength to finish it. In the 1983 Oberon anthology, Sandra Martin and I published a Marian Engel story called "Blue Glass and Flowers" in which the central character struggles to come to terms with an inevitable death. The character was not in any simple sense autobiographical, but obviously the story grew from the overwhelming challenge that Marian was facing.

"You only get one death," the woman observes, "and it's up to you to do it well."

About that time, Marian received a small legacy, and with some of the money, she decided to have the garden of her house in Toronto landscaped and improved. She was having increasing difficulty getting around and she had decided to make a place that was beautiful and calm and suitable for contemplation. It was one way of trying to "do it well."

"Under the Hill," which is published in this collection, is one of her last stories and clearly grew out of whatever serenity she was able to achieve. In it she returns to the not-always-loved people of her childhood, the severe, wilful people of rural southwestern Ontario, and finds there a magical, unexpected beauty.

In the face of death, she offers human kindness, and flowers.

DAVID HELWIG

Contributions for the sixteenth volume, published or unpublished, should be sent to the editors, David Helwig and Sandra Martin, at 106 Montreal Street, Kingston, Ontario, K7K 3E8 before 30 November 1985. All manuscripts should be accompanied by a stamped self-addressed envelope.

6

At Mrs. Warder's House

Edna Alford

From the kitchen window above the sink I can keep an eye on Eric and his friends while I work. I see Stephen Willis is wearing a poppy today, pinned to the chest of his blue-and-white striped muscle shirt. Mrs. Willis should be shot. It's too cold today to be sending a four-year-old boy out to play in a shirt with no sleeves, and the poppy has an open pin, which is a foolish thing to be sticking on a little boy.

Same thing every year. Passing poppies. They'll never learn. Stephen's poppy irritates me, reminds me they must be holding Remembrance Day services in schools all across the country. I was the one most years chosen to read the poem at the service—

In Flanders' Fields the poppies blow
Between the crosses row on row
That mark our place…

There can't be many of us who don't know the words by now, after all the shuffling dusty afternoons, squirming on hard-backed stacking-chairs, itching to get out and rip off the sad little red velvet cardboard corsage with the black felt dot for a centre, to rid ourselves of the pitiful poppy which, along with the teachers, the compulsory minister and the Veterans' Affairs Department, conspired to make us all feel the sorrowful same—which we would not do.

The teachers said they chose me for my voice because it carried, and I knew the implication was that I should be honoured. But for me it was no honour. For one thing it separated me from my friends. I had to sit on the platform with the minister and the pianist. I could see my friends, their pony-tails bobbing silly in the distance. And I was given to giggling back then, spent a fair amount of my platform time trying to control it.

The other reason I could feel no honour in having been chosen was because I knew I didn't deserve it. Because I knew what I was supposed to feel when I didn't. I had no excuse. I had felt it many times before, once at Mrs. Warder's house and the rest of the times with my grandmother. So if my schoolmates remember my solemn face, small and white, surrounded with a wreath of curls, my poppy red and lying for me on the lapel of my best white blouse, they recall a fraudulent respect, a sadness in my round white eyes that was not sorrow, but guilt.

Now, I'm a Certified Accountant and I work full-time for one of the largest accounting firms in Alberta. I consider myself highly competent, but I'd be the first to admit having trouble coping with the double day, as they call it—eight at work and eight at home. I save most of my housework for weekends and, as usual, I seem to be spending half of it at the kitchen sink, which is not ordinarily this unpleasant. I can look out the window and listen to the radio while I work. Sometimes I even sing along, "If I were a carpenter, and you were a lady, would you marry me anyway, would you have my babies..."

It's not just the poppies. It's other things. Like the berry blood my small son brings in on his hands, squeezed crimson dye from fallen clusters underneath the mountain ash in our back yard. And the hedge of cotoneaster lying like a wreath around my neighbour's yard, the leaves all speckled red and gold from early frost. And for some reason, voices always seem to carry farther in the fall. Maybe that has something to do with it. I feel this way every year when the leaves are not quite gone, like thinning hair on men. Sometimes it's later; sometimes no leaves at all by the time I get around to it. But always and eventually, I do remember Mrs. Warder's house.

This morning I put down twelve more quarts of pickles. Beets this time. A part of my past I can't seem to let go of, although I know I have no time for this sort of thing anymore and the accountant in me says I don't really save any money with the cost of sugar and jars these days, and my time into the bargain. But it's a kind of compulsion with me, makes me feel right somehow, putting things down for the winter, making provision. Ritual. My mother, her mother, her mother's mother— God knows how far back it goes. As far back as there is, I guess, for women. At least as far back as honouring the battle dead.

Beets are messy though. For some reason I always forget from one year to the next that they bleed all over everything, stain the white arborite on the counter-top, dye the wooden spoons a colour not unlike menstrual blood. And now I'm faced with cleaning up the mess again, scouring the stains from pots and spoons and saying—Jesus Christ why am I doing this—some people never learn—half mutter, half chant, always a little surprised by the comfort that comes from the repetition, even of curses or bad news.

The news is over. The tone signal. The time. The twelve o'clock news. It is worse every time I listen. The broadcaster just said the situation in the Middle East is so serious the United States government is asking all American men and women of military age to register with their nearest draft-board office. Now they're calling women. I try to put it out of my mind, try not to think about it. But the season works against me, the cold clear air coming in through the kitchen window. Now they're calling women. The possibility exists, no matter how I try to avoid it. I might be called up someday. Not soon, I know that, but someday maybe. "Called up" as my mother used to say. "Your Uncle Olaf was called up," she'd say. Her brother. "After he was called up, he never came home. We never saw him again." Irrational, of course. Then, it didn't necessarily follow that being called up meant you never came home. I know lots of men who served, men in my father's generation, my father himself.

The worst of it is there are women willing enough to go. So we all edge toward the front line, wherever that may be in this day and age, rather more like a ball of yarn, I suspect, than a line, intersect and then around, intersect and then around and around and around.

Ordinarily I like to look out the window. But Stephen's silly poppy aggravates me. Even the sight of

Eric himself, crouched under the mountain ash, makes me angry. Eric has straight blond hair. "A perfect Aryan," my husband once said, half joking (he is, after all, half German), "except the hair will never lie exactly flat—maybe he's safe." The window is open and I can hear their conversation under the tree begin, quietly at first.

"Do you know my guinea pig got killed?" asks Stephen.

"Who killed him?" says Eric.

"I don't know. He just got murdered. My mom found him by the fence. He got a wire stuck in his stomach and he just got dead."

"And blooded?" asks Eric, with too much enthusiasm for my liking. "And did his bones get squashed?"

"I don't know. No, I don't think so. I think he just got a wire stuck in his stomach and he just got dead."

"But how did he get dead?" Eric pursues.

Stephen is hollering now. "I don't know I said. I said he just got killed, that's all I said. He just got murdered." He picks up a stick. And Eric picks up a rock lying in the circle of dirt under the tree.

"Hey, hey, hey," I call out through the open window. "No more of that, you guys." Both of them look up at the window, surprised they are not alone, curiously surprised they are being watched. Stephen puts down his stick and Eric throws his rock over the back fence.

I look down at my hands, limp in the sink, the water a cloudy burgundy now from the beet juice. I'm a little startled by the colour, not so much by the colour itself as by the fact that I've been wallowing in it for almost twenty minutes without noticing the colour. Mindless. Up to my elbows in dishwater again. Which may be the main reason I started to think about Mrs. Warder. She always smelled of soap. Not Ivory Snow, not gentle fragrant soap. Sharp soap. Lye. Which I remember reading somewhere is used sometimes to cover uncoffined corpses, outside prisons, I think it was, or in wars. Why I don't know. The reason wasn't really given. But it's lye soap I remember at Mrs. Warder's house.

Mrs. Warder lived in Trestle. She's dead now, but she used to live on a sidestreet in a small house the shape of a chicken-coop, grey clapboard with a roof that slanted from the front to the back. The house was fenced with chicken-wire. I used to go there with my grandmother sometimes when I was on summer holidays.

Mrs. Warder's house was surrounded with poppies, squat orange California poppies sprinkled with babies' breath, pretty really, if you like that sort of thing. And closer to the house were great red opium poppies opened up so wide I could see their throats, wide as if they were screaming something I couldn't hear. And over the house itself, a blanket of lobelia, small purple flowers on a bed of scalloped leaves, climbing in vines up the ladder of lumber till they almost touched the roof. I used to wonder what would happen when they crawled up over the top, what it was they could see from Mrs. Warder's roof that would make the climb worthwhile.

These purple blossoms everywhere on green were vaguely shaped like valentines, not exact, like the ones I cut out of books in February, not symmetrical, each one just different enough for me to see that they were not the same, though all of them were purple. At school, we had been learning about the body in Health Class—the skeleton, the lungs, that sort of thing. And the last lesson before summer holidays that year had been on the heart, and when I looked up at Mrs. Warder's vine-covered porch, I couldn't help thinking of all the blood those purple flowers must have known had they been hearts.

My grandmother and I walked over to Mrs. Warder's house. It wasn't far from Aunt Ida's where we stayed, only down the ravine, across the highway, then the main street and down two blocks. I don't believe they named the streets in Trestle back then, or if they did, I never knew. There were a lot of things I never noticed then. For instance, years later, I learned from cousins that everyone in town said Mrs. Warder had bats in her belfry. They told me she threw pots and pans at any of the kids who came near the house. Whacky Warder, they used to call her. But I still find that hard to believe because she was always so good to me when I went there with my grandmother.

We both had to get all dressed up to go—me in my lilac taffeta and her in her rose print with her silver shell brooch from Norway. And a hat. A pink straw pillbox with two small red rosebuds on a silk band. Her hair was already completely white. I held her hand when we walked over there even then, though I must have been ten or eleven years old by that time.

When we got there we went in through the gate and to the back door. We stood on the stoop and Grandma knocked. When Mrs. Warder came to the door, she smiled, flapped open the screen door and hugged me hard, which I didn't like. She smelled so strong of soap.

"Hedvig!" she said to my grandmother. "Come in, come on in." Mrs. Warder was fat and had a round face. She wore a dark brown hair-net over grey pin curls and some of the bobby-pins stuck out of the net, making her look a little like a porcupine, like an illustration out of Beatrix Potter. She wore an immaculate full white apron.

Her whole house smelled of lye soap and cabbage. She led us through the kitchen to the living-room, small and full of doilies and china dogs and icebox flowers. The far wall was hung with pictures. A baby picture in a small oval silver frame. A Boy Scout picture, a pale adolescent hand raised in a two-finger salute, like the Scouts at school on Remembrance Day. A high-school graduation picture, still a boy, I remember, a round fat face framed with one of those black hats with the diamond cardboard tops. And centred among these, a large, tinted, ornately framed photograph of a young man in uniform with wings on the shoulders. I distinctly remember the wings.

I sat on the couch across from the photograph wall and looked at them or rather at him. You could hardly do otherwise at Mrs. Warder's house because the couch and two chairs were arranged in such a way in the tiny room that you really had no choice. If you didn't look at the photographs, you pretty well had to look at your shoes. Now I recognize this to be the nature of shrines, this uncanny ability of making you bow your head without even knowing why.

Grandma and Mrs. Warder sat at a round oak pedestal table in the corner. Mrs. Warder picked up a pencil and continued work on a crossword puzzle left unfinished when she had come to the door. At the time this didn't seem peculiar to me, I suppose because my grandma seemed to accept it as a natural course for the visit to take, as if she had been through it before. Grandma sat and watched her for a while. They didn't speak. Nor did I. And time suspended itself, as it sometimes seems to do, out of neglect, I often think, or maybe in this case out of an awareness of its own silliness, of how little difference it really made, in this house in particular.

Pretty soon Mrs. Warder looked up at Grandma and said, "What's a seven-letter word for forgetting, Hedvig?"

"Forgetting what, Frieda?" Grandma said.

"Forgetting everything," Mrs. Warder replied and smiled. "You know. Like what happened to the boys overseas. Olaf and Carl."

"Oh dat," said Grandma, remembering, "Amneesha."

"That's it," Mrs. Warder said. "Only it's not 'amneesha,' Hedvig, it's 'am-ne-si-a.' Isn't that so Irene?" She looked at me. "Am-ne-si-a," she repeated, "you're a clever little girl. I'll bet you can spell 'am-ne-si-a.'"

"No," I said, "I can't. I don't know that word. We never took it yet."

"Well it's where a person loses all his memory, you know. Like Carl and Olaf, in the war. So's they can't remember who they are or where they come from. Even who their mothers are. So's they have to start all over again. In England, say, or somewhere overseas. You think they're back in England, Hedvig?"

"Vell, dat could be I guess," Grandma said quietly.

I couldn't believe my ears. I had spent every Remembrance Day since Grade 1 with my grandmother. In Saskatoon. In the morning we went to the parade and the service at the cenotaph where all the soldiers were. We watched them lay the wreath. We wore our poppies. We walked back to her room in the Ross Block on Third Avenue by the old Eaton's and we sat together for the rest of the day. She crocheted and I read or played with her jewellery, all of it except for the silver cross in the black velvet box, which was empty today because the cross was pinned to her grey wool coat. Sometimes when I got really bored, I would sit by the window watching the traffic moving below on Third Avenue. The cars were sparse because Remembrance Day was a statutory holiday then, everywhere, for everyone.

Toward late afternoon, usually just as it was getting dark, early in November, she would get the pictures out. They were in an album she kept in a small cupboard by the radiator. She kept her books of Norway here as well, and I always got to look at them too, which was good because they were full of beautiful pictures of fjords and blossoms and boats. We looked at these books first, a ritual we had of pretending to go over everything and just

15

happening upon what I now call the real pictures, the pictures of Uncle Olaf on a horse in front of a granary when he was a boy, tow-headed, like Eric. And Uncle Gunar who died of diptheria when he was four on my grandparents first homestead near Viscount.

The picture of Gunar was strange, old and yellow—a picture of a miniature coffin with a window in the top. And through the window I could see the boy in a white embroidered bonnet and the top of a white embroidered nightie, which I now realize must have been his christening gown.

She held the picture in her lap for a long time, not even looking at it. I guess after all that time she didn't have to, had it somewhere in her head more clear than what was left on cardboard. And then she moved to those of Olaf and did the same. Held them each in turn for what seemed like a long time to me then, although it must only have been minutes. And finally she wept, head up, eyes open, making no sound. The only way I could tell in the half-dark was by the water on her face, illuminated red and green at regular intervals by the revolving neon sign of Day's Paint and Wallpaper attached to the brick wall beneath her window. Even then I knew she wept for both, indiscriminately. The one she'd lost through pestilence, the one through war. It didn't seem to make any difference to her how they'd died.

Those nights, she always let me stay up late, and when the cenotaph clock struck eleven, she turned on her television set and we sat and watched the CBC news. Every year the same. Some mother unearthed somewhere in the country who had lost two, three, maybe even four sons. They always had her lay a wreath in Ottawa at the cenotaph there and I got this idea that there were cenotaphs everywhere you went, like houses or like churches, everywhere you go.

I nearly spoke at Mrs. Warder's house, in that matter-of-fact way children sometimes have of speaking. I almost said, "They're dead. My Uncle Olaf and Gunar too—and Carl. My grandma told me so."

But Mrs. Warder said she thought they'd make out pretty well. "Carl was always so clever," she said. "He won every trophy Trestle High School had to offer. And it was worth the effort. That's what I always told him," she said, "every bit of the work is worth the effort. When he got low and wondered what he'd do and where he'd get the money to go to the city for university. And why he studied so hard anyway and wasn't out there with the rest kicking up his heels. 'It's worth every bit of the effort,' I told him—and you should remember that too, Irene," she said turning her head and nodding at the couch where I sat, bored to tears, my hands limp and sweaty in my lap. "And I said it to myself too, Hedvig," she continued, "when I was up on the hill scrubbing out Mrs. Carling's kitchen, down on my hands and knees. I always said I'd scrub every floor in Trestle a thousand times over if I thought it would help him along. And I know he's doing fine, Hedvig. And your boy, Olaf," she reached across the table and touched my grandmother's arm. "I know he'll make his way. He was always so good with his hands, Hedvig, and you couldn't hope to meet a lad more thoughtful. They're probably married by now," she said and smiled. "You think they might have kids?"

"Ja, I imagine so," Grandma said without blinking, without so much as a hint to Mrs. Warder or to me that there was any doubt. They both had kids. I was dumbfounded.

Mrs. Warder served us tea, which tasted as if it were brewed with bath-salts, and scooped Neapolitan ice cream out of a waxy brick, half-thawed and sudsy on the outer edges. It tasted old and awful. After tea I watched them play Canasta until it was time to go.

On the way home I held my grandmother's hand. By the time we reached the boardwalk crossing the ravine, I had made up my mind I would ask her. "Why does Mrs. Warder smell like soap?" I said, sneaking a look up at her soft white face.

"Ssst," Grandma said.

Then, "Why doesn't she keep her ice cream in the fridge like other people do?"

"She doesn't hef one."

"But why does she think—"

"Ssst." She looked down at me quickly, her face a flat iron square, and she squeezed my hand hard, a hurting hard I thought had broken fingers. But I never forgot and I never asked or thought of asking the question again. I guess I didn't really need to because I knew, right from that time forward—things can get so bad you can't forget them; sometimes they get so bad you can't remember. She must have thought I was too young to know and even if I did, too young to remember. But children do. They do remember. And for me it always comes back this time of year, each day a little shorter, each night a little darker than the last.

It's worse this year, for some reason. The news maybe. It certainly doesn't help to listen to the news. And Eric throwing rocks, of all things. I've never seen him do it before. They say all kids try it but it took me by surprise, a boy who still needs to be rocked to sleep sometimes— throwing stones.

I lift the stopper out of the sink and watch the water, coagulated dark and soapy, circle down the drain. Eric has just come in from outside. He looks cold. His cheeks are red. I should have put a jacket on him.

"Stephen's guinea pig got tooken to God's Jesus!" he shouts, exultant.

"I doubt that very much, Eric." This comes out too sharp, I know. I dry my hands on a tea-towel hanging on the oven door and bend down to kiss him. His flesh is cold and I draw back. I can smell the rotting leaves in his sweater. The fall. It's all around him. Seems somehow inside him. He holds a cluster of smashed berries in his hands. They're smeared on his shoes and I can see where he has tracked them in sticky patches all across my freshly scrubbed floor.

"Get into the bathroom and get that mess cleaned up," I yell, "and don't you ever bring any of those stupid things into this house again." I grab a spatula from the cutlery holder in the drying-rack and almost throw it, watch it in my mind slow motion hurtle end over end awkward through the air, clatter against the far wall of the kitchen and drop to the floor. I can't believe I almost threw it, look down at the kitchen tool, at my hand, inspect it as if it belonged to someone else, as if I were looking for an injury of some kind. And then I begin to pound the soft edge of the hand against the sharp edge of the counter, pounding and pounding till the hand slips and knocks over the box of soap sitting too close to the edge. The soap flakes spill over the counter-edge like a waterfall of snow, forming a small mound on the linoleum and spraying around my feet.

Eric and I both watch the last flakes trickle over the edge. Then, still looking at the floor, I step out of my own footprints. When I look up my eyes meet his. Ordinarily he would have laughed. We both would have. The footprints are so clear, like cartoon steps, the kind you see pasted on sidewalks as a joke, leading nowhere. But he doesn't laugh. His eyes are frightened and confused, as if I were watching him with Mrs. Warder's eyes, as if he were afraid I'd pick up the coffee-pot next, or the Dutch oven.

"It's only berries, Mom," he says finally, trying to

19

defend himself against something he has no way of knowing, "just berries."

Irene, I tell myself, he just turned four. He's four years old, for Christ's sake, like Gunar in the little box. And I want to tell him it has nothing to do with berries, nothing to do with kitchen floors. Most of all I want to tell myself it has nothing to do with me or the smell of lye soap or pinning poppies on the clothes of my children. But I don't have to say anything. He runs up to me and grabs me round the leg and I take his head in my hands and press it hard against me. He doesn't cry. He is too scared. But I begin, the water moving slow and cold over the skin on my face.

"Get into the bathroom," I say again, quietly this time, "and wash yourself."

Dulce

Jane Rule

I was not perfectly born, as Samuel Butler prescribed, wrapped in banknotes, but I was orphaned at 21 without other relatives to turn to and with no material need of them. I was, in a way everyone else envied, free of emotional and financial obligations. I did not have to do anything, not even choose a place to live since I had the small and lovely house in Vancouver where I had grown up to shelter me from as much as developing my own taste in furniture. I did not, of course, feel fortunate. Ingratitude is the besetting sin of the young.

If I had been rich rather than simply comfortable, I might have learned to give my money away intelligently. What I tried to do instead was to give myself away, having no use of my own for it. It was not so reprehensible an aim for a young woman in the fifties as it is today. I was, again with a good fortune I was far from recognizing, unsuccessful.

My first and greatest insight as a child was being aware that I was innocent of my own motives. I did not know why I so often contrived to interrupt my father at his practising. Now I understand that he, otherwise a quiet and pensive man, frightened me when he played his violin. Or the instrument itself frightened me, seeming to contain an electrical charge that flung my father's body around helplessly the moment he laid hands on it. Though he died in a plane crash on tour for the troops in the Second World War when I was fifteen, I never quite believed it wasn't his violin that had killed him.

Wilson C. Wilson, a boy several years older than I, lived down the block with his aunt and uncle who gave him dutiful but reluctant room among their own children because he had been orphaned as a baby. That fact, accompanied by his dark good looks, had made him a romantic figure for me, but I had never expected him to climb up into our steep north slope of a garden where I made a habit of brooding on a favourite rock and often spying on him through the fringe of laurel, dogwood, mountain ash and alder that grew, and still does grow, down at the street. No handsome boy of my own age had ever paid the slightest attention to me.

If he had not come with such quick agility, I would have hidden from him and let him pay his respects to my grieving mother to whom I suspect he might have been more romantically drawn than he was to me. I was too terrified of him even to be self-conscious. I sat very still, hardly at first hearing what he had to say, waiting for him to leave, but he was so gentle with me and at the same time so eager that gradually I began to listen to him.

"Some day," he said, "you'll be glad you were old enough to remember his face."

He offered his own grief as a way of sharing mine, but I had not had time to let my raw loss mellow into something speakable. He did not expect me to be adequate then or, I suppose, ever.

After that, once or twice a week he would come to find me. Sometimes he talked about his weekend job as an apprentice to a printer, but more often he talked about the books he was reading. He did not expect me to be older or more intelligent than I was, but he did begin to bring me books to read. When I asked him a question that pleased him, he would say, "Dulce, you have an old soul," but he was normally content to have a good listener.

Sometimes he suggested a walk on the beach just several blocks below the house, even in winter weather. We both liked the mists that obscured the far views across Burrard Inlet to the north mountains and focused our attention on the salty debris at our feet. We liked finding puzzling objects and making up histories for them as we walked among gulls and crows, past ghostly trees emerging only a few feet from us.

Neither of us liked wearing a hat or hood, and we would come back as wet-headed as swimmers to a hearth fire and tea, to the personal questions my mother asked, which always began, "If you don't have to go..." or "If you're not called up..." or "If the war's over..." I never asked Wilson questions like that though I could see my mother's concern for his peaceful future gave him more confidence in it. He wanted to go back to Toronto where he had been born. He wanted to study literature and philosophy.

"And after that?" Mother asked.

"I'll be a philosopher...and a printer to feed myself."

I watched him, his strong, dark hair glistening rather than flattened, as I knew mine was, by the damp, his dark eyes glistening, too, and wished he were my brother or at least in some way related to me.

Wilson was called up two weeks before the war was over. Then his orders were cancelled, and he packed instead to go to Toronto. Before he left, he asked for my picture in exchange for his, taken for his high-school graduation, on which he had written, "For a good listener, Wilson C. Wilson."

"I so dislike my name," he once told me, "that I'll simply have to make it famous."

"How?"

He shrugged, but I wasn't really surprised when he sent me the first of his poems to be published in an eastern magazine. Some few of the images in them were ones we had found together, which made it easier for me to comment on them. Now that we were exchanging letters, I discovered that being a good listener by mail was learning to ask interesting rather than personal questions.

When Wilson came back the following summer to take up work with the printer, his aunt and uncle asked him to pay room and board. I was shocked by their lack of generosity, particularly since it would mean Wilson could not afford to go east again.

"My uncle points out that my cousins are perfectly satisfied to go to UBC."

"He doesn't charge them room and board, does he?"

"They're his own children," Wilson explained reasonably.

"You could pitch a tent in our garden," I suggested, "and you could pay Mother just the bit it cost to feed you."

"Don't make offers for your mother," he said.

"Are you in love with Wilson?" my mother asked me.

"I don't think so," I answered, both surprised and embarrassed by the question. "I just want us to help him."

"Is he in love with you?"

That I knew was preposterous. "I'm just a good listener," I answered.

The tent did go up on the flat square of lawn by the roses on the understanding that I would not visit Wilson in it. I would not have dreamed of invading his privacy.

More like a grown man, he assigned himself chores about the place without being asked. Mother and I had been used to a man who protected his hands and anyway had no eye or ear for the complaints of a house. By the end of the summer, nothing squeaked or dripped, and I had decided to go away to college myself and major in English.

I liked the idea of a women's college, for boys, except for Wilson, began to alarm me, taking on sudden height all around me, their noses and fingers thickening, their chins growing mossy, their voices cracking to new depths. I walked as defensively among them as I would through thickets of gorse or blackberry.

I chose Mills College in California partly because it was in the Bay Area, and I liked San Francisco, the city of my mother's girlhood. Though my mother had been sent to the Conservatory of Music and attended concerts with her handsome and handsomely dressed parents, they hadn't approved of her marriage to a fellow student who wanted to sit on the stage instead of in the prosperous audience.

"They said, 'he'll never buy you diamonds,'" my mother told me.

"Did you mind?"

"About the diamonds?"

"About their not approving."

"Yes, but it gave me the courage to do it."

I found it hard to associate courage with love.

Wilson did not come back to Vancouver the summer I graduated from high school. He had found a printing job in Toronto, a less expensive solution than living in a tent in our garden. I sent him my high-school graduation picture without signing it because I didn't know what to say. I signed my letters "As ever." He signed his "Yours," which I understood to be a formality.

Two of the poems he had published that year were love poems, dark and constrained, which made me unhappy for him and a little bewildered, too, for I could not imagine anyone incapable of returning his love. Since he wasn't in the habit of confiding in me about his personal affairs, I could hardly answer or question a poem. He wrote to me that his first collection of poems was about to be published, sent me the picture to be used on the cover and asked permission to dedicate the book to me.

"Does it mean anything, Mother? I mean, anything in particular?"

"It's not a proposal, if that's what you mean," Mother said. "But it certainly does mean you are important to him. It's all right to accept if he's important to you."

I accepted, feeling a new self-conscious place in his life, which I did not really understand. Surely, if he'd been in love with me, I would know. I studied the picture and saw simply his familiar intent and handsome face. Experimentally I kissed it, a kiss as chaste as any I gave my mother. Then quite crossly I thought, "If I'm so important to him, he could at least have come to my graduation and taken me to the dance."

Yet who of my school friends could boast of having a book dedicated to her? Wilson would never have taken me to a dance. Nor would I have asked him to. He did not belong to my silly social world. Even I had outgrown it and longed to begin my own serious education in a part of the world nearly as beautiful and far more sophisticated than my own.

To the relief of some of my disgruntled, liberal professors, I shunned the child development and dietary courses newly introduced to make servantless wives out of my post-war generation and to redomesticate those few female veterans who had returned. Instead I chose traditional art history, religious history and philosophy courses as electives around my requirements in literature. If there had been a history of science, I would have chosen that over biology, the least mathematical of the sciences available. In that lab, cutting up flat worms, crayfish and cats, I came as close to domestic experience as I would get in college. I sent my laundry out every week to a war widow, left not as well off as my mother.

Thanks to Wilson, I was better read than many of the other incoming freshmen, and, though I rarely offered an opinion in class, I asked very good questions. My written assignments were not immediately successful, but again Wilson had trained me to listen and comprehend not only the material but the mood and bias of the instructor before me. Once I got the hang of being a logical positivist in philosophy, a new critic in contemporary literature, a propounder of history of ideas in Milton, my grades bounded upwards.

There were students at the college who actually engaged in the arts, notably in music, but I avoided the rich offering of concerts. In fact, any performing art was difficult for me to deal with; for, like my father, the performers all seemed in the grip of an energy that made spastic victims of them, leaping inexplicably around the stage, shouting in unrecognizable voices, faces either

27

entirely expressionless or distorted in unimaginable pain. Poetry was for me a superior art. I had never had to watch Wilson write a poem. It was a relief to me to study Shakespeare on the page, a prejudice I shared with my professor who considered any available production a defiler of the poetry of the bard.

At a performance of *Macbeth,* put on by St. Mary's, a men's college in the neighbourhood, the wife of a faculty member played Lady Macbeth in the same red housecoat even after she'd become queen; the wind for the witches' scene was her vacuum cleaner. Macbeth himself was a speech major with a lisp, who murdered more than sleep. His severed head was presented at the end of the play in a paper bag that looked like someone's forgotten lunch and perhaps was.

Granting the limitations of amateurs, I could not imagine even great actors tastefully gouging out eyes on stage on the way to a climax of corpses. The blood and gore were a convention of a barbarous time, which the poetry transcended.

In my letters to Wilson, both of whose pictures sat framed on my desk, I sometimes confided academic puzzlement. Though styles of poetry changed through the ages, particular poems were recognizably great in each period. Prose, on the other hand, seemed to improve, become more economical, lucid and beautiful. "Are you going to make an idol out of Hemingway," Wilson demanded, "at the expense of Donne and Milton?" I'd had F. Scott Fitzgerald in mind. I went back to Donne's sermons, and, when I imaged them, as instructed by Wilson, recited by the Dean of St. Paul's with tears streaming down his face, their excesses seemed more appropriate; yet I also had to admit that a man in tears would embarrass more than move me.

I found few fellow students with whom I could raise

such questions. Only a small band of rather aggressive scholarship students discussed their studies. The more acceptable topics of conversation were menstrual cramps, other people's sexual habits, the foibles of parents and professors, and God. Nor were academic subjects acceptable topics on dates. Any conversation was impossible over the noise at fraternity parties, football games and bars. The only virtue of the gross abuse of alcohol at such gatherings was that, more often than not, my young man of the evening was incapable of a sexual ending in the back seat of a dangerously driven car.

At first I was uneasy at the status my pictures of Wilson gave me. When I confessed that he had also dedicated a book of poems to me, it was simply assumed hat I was unofficially engaged to the handsome young man with the unhandsome name. He wrote me letters, which was more than could be said for some who had even presented diamond rings.

"Are you going to see Wilson at Christmas?"

"Oh, he probably can't afford the trip. He's putting himself through..."

Explanations true enough, but I did not think of myself as the object of Wilson's romantic interest. There were more love poems, flickering with unredeeming fire that certainly had nothing to do with me, but they gave rise to shocked and admiring speculations among my friends who read them.

Gradually I used Wilson as the protection I wanted from a social life too barbarous to bear, even if it meant remaining among the humiliated on Saturday nights. If I was not writing love letters to Wilson, I was writing loving ones, for he was the one human being, aside from my mother, with whom I could really talk.

To Wilson's great disappointment, the only fellowship open to him for graduate studies was at UBC. He frankly confessed that it would be all right with him if he never laid eyes on Vancouver again. The university was inferior, the city really not a city at all, for it was without cultural reality, and he had been personally unhappy there. He did kindly add, "Except for that summer in your garden." But he was competing with too many men older than himself, more mature in their judgments, with Americans and Englishmen as well as his own countrymen, and he had to take what he could get.

Wilson met me at the airport when I came home to bury my mother. It was the first time we had seen each other in four years, and we embraced in the way we signed our letters because we had to do something. Wilson seemed to me more substantial and attentive in those few days, but my need was also extraordinary. It was Wilson who would not hear of my simply staying there, moving into the house to begin a grief-dazed life. He put me back on the plane to finish my education.

In the next year and a half, Wilson became my unofficial guardian. He rented the house for me, effectively preventing me from coming home in the summer, which he said I should spend in Europe where he had not yet been himself.

He outlined a trip he would like to have taken, but I was far too timid to travel alone, and, since he didn't offer to come with me, I elected instead to take the Shakespeare summer session at Stratford.

Younger than most of the other international students and not as well prepared for the work, I was at first intimidated, but my listening, question-asking habits soon provided me with a couple of unofficial tutors, also willing to indulge my uncertain sensibilities about the theatre.

"Why, it's meant to be vulgar!" I exclaimed after a performance of *Measure for Measure*. "All that bawdy fooling around."

If it hadn't been for Wilson, I might have fallen in love with either of the two young men, one English, one American, who also took me punting on the Avon, day tripping to Oxford, to Wales, pub crawling and simply walking country lanes in the late summer light. While both of them talked nearly as well as Wilson about matters literary and historical, they were also flirtatious and entertaining. Instead I fell in love with England and wrote to tell Wilson that we had both been born on the wrong continent. We were not after all freaks, simply freaks in the new world.

'This bloke of yours back in Canada, are you going to marry him then?" the Englishman asked.

"Oh, eventually," I answered, and I found that I believed what I said.

I spent my final year at college in a postponing aura of serene industry, my essays enlivened by new insights that were my own, for I had been in that green and pleasant land and knew that birds do sing.

But at last I did have to go home to discover that my mother really was dead, that I was alone. If the house had been on an ordinary street in an ordinary city, I might have been persuaded to sell it and live the more vagabond life of my contemporaries, brash and brave among the new ruins of Europe, before returning to mow lawns and pay taxes. But it was built sturdily on a high piece of ground overlooking the inlet, the mountains and the growing city of Vancouver, and it contained my childhood, which was prematurely precious to me as my parents were.

Wilson had not met my plane, nor did he come to see me until I'd had several days of blank passivity. I did not think it odd at the time. When he did arrive, I greeted him less shyly than before and felt him pull back. His

Dulce was still not a woman but a docile, intelligent child in need of his guidance.

I could not ask him, as I very much wanted to, "What are we going to do with the rest of our lives?" He considered his to be publicly disposed, as a poet and teacher. He would give up printing, though he might one day use that practical knowledge if he founded a literary press.

"Vancouver is changing," Wilson admitted as we looked together at the view, the skyline altered by the first of so many high-rises that would eventually make it look more like New York than itself.

Then he asked, as if an uninvolved spectator, "What are you going to do now?"

"I don't know."

"You haven't thought about it?"

"I wondered if I'd get a dog...no, I haven't."

"Why?"

"Do I have to do anything?"

"Well, eventually," Wilson said. "You haven't got enough capital to live on, not the way you'd like to live."

I was furious with him for speaking as if I might never marry him or anyone else: yet I knew he would think it beneath me to leave my life to such an eventuality. I must be held accountable for my future.

All the girls I had known at school were either locked in combat with their parents or already married. Only two had jobs, chosen for their proximity to marriageable men, which, of course, Wilson was not and would not be for some time until he could translate his years of learning into a modest academic salary. If I had to mark time until then, I might as well do it with him. I could get a teaching assistantship and take my MA.

At first, witness to all the fawning young women who surrounded Wilson, I was both daunted and repelled, but, as I watched him treat them like bodies on a crowded bus, I was reassured. He was a little aloof from me, too, at first, as if he did not want any display of our friendship, but gradually we formed the habit of having lunch together several times a week. For his birthday, I gave him season tickets next to my own for the theatre and the foreign film series. We became in public, rather than in private, a pair.

Wilson had rooms in a widow's house on the second floor with only a hotplate to cook on and a glimpse of view through a small, stained-glass window in his bathroom, which I saw only in the lines of one of his poems. He never invited me there, in deference to the widow's sensibilities perhaps but in keeping with his appetite for privacy.

He visited me comfortably enough, and he did the same things for me as he had done for Mother as well as advising me about my responsibilities as an owner. But we almost always went out after the simple meals I was learning to prepare under his direction and with his help.

To my relief, Wilson did not want to go to poetry readings. He said he had nothing in common with the other students who claimed to be poets and brought out a magazine called *Tish*. "It's not really necessary to spell it backwards," Wilson said. To focus on the human breath and the heartbeat for a theory of aesthetics was simply an excuse to ignore the great traditions of poetry. For Wilson the roots of poetry were in knowledge, discipline and concentration. He admired Auden, Eliot, the best of Dylan Thomas, a good reason for avoiding the drunken bellowings of that undersized bull on the stage. About giving readings of his own, Wilson was non-committal. "I'm not ready."

We went instead to the Art Gallery for every visiting show. Wilson was fascinated by the question of great subjects. I was more interested in paint and stone and metal; therefore I didn't have the trouble with modern art that often daunted Wilson, fearful of being tricked by fads and imposters. How could he judge technique without subject matter, he wanted to know. "Think of it as more like music," I suggested.

When he went with me to openings at local galleries, Wilson stood back from the conversations I got into, I suppose because he was more comfortable with answers than with questions, but he did listen, and occasionally he would go with me to parties held after the shows for the artist and his friends.

Wilson would have preferred me to invest in something like first editions, about which he was relatively well informed, but the only first editions I've ever bought are new books. I have no taste for books as objects. What I wanted were paintings. For me they were as pure as poems.

In asserting that aesthetic independence, I did not feel so much Wilson's equal as a better, more independent companion, one he would some day come to see as a woman rather than a fifteen-year-old with an old soul. He dedicated his second book of poems to me with the words, "For Dulce, my muse."

Just the other day I came upon a metaphorical distinction between the romantic and classical poets in Northrop Frye: "Warm mammalians who tenderly suckle their living creations and the cold reptilian intellectuals who lay abstract eggs." There were no love poems at all in this second collection. Like the canvases Wilson was drawn to, they were about great subjects. The title came from the longest and most difficult poem in the book, *Exercises in War.* Trained as I had been, it didn't occur to me to wonder whether or not I liked Wilson's poetry. I admired it as intellectually requiring and courageously cruel about the nature of man.

Three months before Wilson received his PhD, he accepted a graduate fellowship in England.

"You'll never come back," I said.

"I hope not."

"Wilson, what about me?"

The eyes he turned to me were brilliant with unshed tears. "I'm sorry, Dulce."

Now that Wilson C. Wilson has made his name attractive with international honours, occasionally a graduate student comes to me to ask what Wilson was like as a young man. I can only say what he tried to be like as a young man in order to become what he now actually is, a very good poet whose poems I can't bear to read.

If Wilson was a coward, he wasn't coward enough to marry me. I was coward enough to have married him to seal myself away forever from learning either to live alone or truly with another. Instead, he left me when I was 24 in the cocoon of my independence, which exposed rather than hid my humiliation, for very soon after Wilson left, Oscar Kaufman, a sculptor at whose studio we had often been, said to me, "I thought at least he'd marry you for the view you've got here."

Perhaps because Oscar was as unlike Wilson as it is possible for a man to be, I was not so much attracted to him as resigned to him for the medicine I needed for a kill or cure remedy for the last ten years of my life.

He was, as most of our friends were in those days, older. Wilson felt safer among people settled in marriage and the raising of children than among other teaching assistants like ourselves who were marrying in nervous numbers and moving into the ugly and cramped married quarters on campus. Perhaps Wilson thought I might be as put off as he obviously was by family life if I could witness first hand the emotional and physical squalor of it.

Oscar and Anita had three children under five years

old. "Catching up after the war," Oscar explained. He was both efficient and tender with them, and he gave Anita a day off every Saturday in exchange for a Saturday night for himself, no questions asked.

When he first stopped by, he had the children with him, and I discovered very quickly how inappropriate my house was for any child neither tied up nor caged. The baby was putting an ant trap in his mouth before anyone had taken a coat off, and Mother's favourite lamp was smashed on the hearth in the next five minutes. After that, Oscar got ahead of them, kid-proofing the room while I got out cookies.

While the children climbed all over him, covering him with enough crumbs to feed every bird in the garden, he said to me, "You know, Dulce, what you've needed for a long time is a real man."

"What's unreal about Wilson?"

"He's a faggot." When I looked blank, Oscar explained, "A queer, a homosexual."

"How do you know such a thing?"

"Don't get mad at *me*," Oscar said. "Do you have any better explanation? Did he ever take you to bed?"

If it hadn't been for the presence of the children, I would have ordered Oscar out of the house. Instead, we both used them as a distraction, and Oscar didn't speak of Wilson again then or ever.

When he had gone, I took down Wilson's first volume of poems and turned to the love poems that had always bewildered me. What I thought had been about unrequited love was instead forbidden, I could quite clearly see, but nothing prevented the reader from supposing the object to be a female, married or otherwise lost to him. It was not, however, a better explanation. Had they been, in a perverse way, poems also for me, the only way Wilson knew how to tell me that he was incapable of loving me?

I had ignored his absolute lack of expressions of physical affection, rationalizing it as part of his extreme sensitivity or a peculiarity of his being raised without tenderness or his sense of honour or some lack in myself because I had loathed those aggressive and drunken young men when I was in college. And I had been relieved that I didn't have to compete with other women for his attention, but there had been no man in his life, of that I was sure. Was Oscar suggesting that Wilson was the kind of man who sought sex in parks and public washrooms? Such an accusation made Oscar rather than Wilson disgusting. If Oscar thought Wilson was queer, why did he also suppose Wilson might have married me?

I try to explain what happened in terms not only of my own ignorance but of the ignorant intolerance of that time. Oh, I had heard rumours of homosexuality in some of Shakespeare's sonnets, but I had dismissed them as I did suggestions that Bacon had really written the plays. I had heard a couple of very masculine girls at college referred to as lesbians, but I associated that with the inappropriateness of their style and manner, rather than with their sexual tastes. The only homosexual male I had ever been aware of was a very effeminate brother of a high-school friend of mine who cried because someone had called him a fairy.

Wilson was entirely masculine. Even in his good looks there was nothing pretty about him. His body was hard and competent, his voice deep. If there was an error in his manner it was an occasional hint of arrogance. There was nothing of the passive or sycophantic about him. He wasn't exactly a man's man either, without interest in either sports or dirty jokes. He was a loner, learning to command respect rather than affection. Yet who could call a man of such intense feelings cold?

I had never pretended to understand Wilson, but he was more real to me than anyone else, both gentler and stronger. My first wish about him, that he could have been my brother, probably most accurately described what we had been for each other and might have gone on being if I had not tried to break the taboo with one question, which created the irrevocable separation and silence between us.

Compared to Wilson, Oscar was transparent, his work hugely, joyously sexual, his needs blatant, his morality patriarchal. He worshipped his wife as the mother of his children; he loved his children, and as a man and an artist he deserved me, but I was also his good deed, part of a sexual altruism he had worked out for himself that drew him to unhappy women. Often in his life he has been bewildered to leave them even unhappier. For some years I let him come to me to be comforted when he was suffering their unreasonable demands and accusations. I can explain that only by my horror at ever again shutting a final door between me and someone I have cared about.

Oscar was from the first completely open with me. Anita didn't mind this sort of thing as long as she didn't have to know about it. His relationship with me was restricted to Saturday nights and would be as entirely private as mine with Wilson had been entirely public. It would end with summer when he was free of his university teaching responsibilities to concentrate on his work. By then I should have become a competent sexual being ready for the open market. No, he didn't put it that way. He was never again blunt as he had been about Wilson. Oscar knew how to be kind and funny about not quite savoury arrangements so that raising any objection seemed a regression to grammar-school morality.

Used to Wilson's spartan taste in food, I was unprepared for Oscar's appetite, and he did not expect to help me in the kitchen or with any other domestic problem. He wanted to leave all husbandly and fatherly responsibilities behind him. He left whatever personal problems he might have had behind him, too. I've never known anyone as resolutely and often maddeningly cheerful as Oscar.

"I made a bargain," he told me once. "If I made it through the war, I'd spend the rest of my life celebrating it."

As he pointed out to me, I could have done worse than to offer my overdue virginity to Oscar. He did not rush me, and he was patient with my timidity and squeamishness. I felt rather like a child being taught to ride a bicycle, that is until *he* mounted *me,* and then I became my father's violin, a thing seemingly of wood and strings, that charged Oscar with crazed energy. I did not know whether I was terrified of him or myself for the power I apparently had to call up such a rutting.

He did not neglect my "pleasure," as he called it, so much as never clearly locate it. From his caresses, I thought I should gradually learn to purr like a cat, but I was too tense in my ignorance to feel the heat he called up as anything more than flashes of ambiguous feeling somewhere between pleasure and pain.

After he left, I often cried hysterically, a response that misled me to think I was in love with Oscar in a way I didn't consciously comprehend, for I also came to dread his arrival on Saturday night, and I was giddy with freedom the few times he was unable to get away.

I did have the sense to refuse Anita's invitation to spend Christmas day with the family. Wilson and I had always planned something to circumvent rather than celebrate that holiday, he not wishing to be politely tolerated in the house where he had grown up, I not wanting to be reminded of the central delight I had been to my parents on such occasions. I had never even explored the cupboard where I supposed the Christmas decorations were stored.

I did what I had wanted to do when I first came home. I went to the Animal Shelter and picked out an already housebroken and spayed young dog, short-haired and black but not as large as a Lab. Then on whim I picked up a black kitten as well. The major part of my Christmas buying, after I'd chosen extravagant presents for Oscar's children (nothing for Oscar at his request), was done in a pet shop.

The dog already had a name, "Rocket," suggesting a male child's brief infatuation with a puppy. I didn't like it, but she was old enough to be used to it. The kitten I named Maud, as all vain, bright and beguiling females should be. From the first night they slept together in the laundry-room by the back door.

Rocket's occasional growl and brief, sharp bark woke me several times during the night. Only someone who has lived years alone can know the absolute pleasure of those animal sounds in the no longer empty house.

"What's this, Dulce?" Oscar exclaimed when Rocket raised her hackles and growled at him and Maud clawed to her highest perch on the bookcase. "A zoo?"

Oscar didn't seem able to like an animal he didn't own. Either Rocket had been abused by a male or she was jealous because, even when I insisted on her good manners, she was sullen about them. She tried to keep herself warm between me and Oscar, and his slightest affectionate gesture started up a hostile singing in her throat. I finally had to tie her up on the back porch, but just as Oscar went into his fit of passion, Rocket began to howl. I had to disengage myself and go speak to her in my firmest tones.

When Oscar left that night, I had hysterical giggles.

"You're turning yourself into a witch," Oscar decided. "Next it will be a black mynah bird."

Neither the image nor the idea of the bird was distasteful to me. But Rocket's continued hostility was becoming a real problem.

"Look, Dulce, you have to get rid of her before you become too attached to her. You can't have a dog around that doesn't like people."

I did not tell him that Rocket was not only polite but quite friendly with the friends I occasionally had in for drinks or dinner, but I did not take Oscar's advice.

Finally he laid down his ultimatum, "Me or that dog."

When I chose the dog, he thought I was joking.

"I know it's shameful to admit it, Oscar, but what I need are pets, not a lover."

"But that's crazy."

I did not argue with him though I knew Rocket and Maud were my first investments in sanity, creatures with whom I could exchange affection and loyalty, about whom I could be ordinarily responsible. How many bad whims and potential disasters can be more simply avoided than with the words, "I have to go home to feed the animals?"

Later I understood that Oscar didn't have the time or energy for more than one woman a winter, and he had to sulk through the rest of that one until he could return to sculpting and to being my friend.

That summer he introduced into his group of huge phallic and pregnant shapes some less voluptuous figures, empty at the centre. I bought one and placed it in the garden by the roses where Wilson had once pitched his impregnable tent.

I would have liked to declare my independence of Wilson's influence by dropping out of the PhD program since there was no longer any point in winning his approval. I was, I think, worried that having such a degree might intimidate another more ordinary sort of man who might make friends with my animals, like my view and marry me. I began research for my thesis simply because I didn't know what else to do.

Conception and development of character fascinated me in Shakespeare where in the early plays crude models of later great characters could be found. Left to myself, I would not have spent months locating other scholars who had noted and explored that subject to see if there were any observations left to be made. But it was a more humane topic than many with teasing application to life.

I wondered if Wilson and Oscar were early, crude models of extremes of male influence in my life or the great characters before whom others would pale. I waffled between a sense that my life was already over and that it had not really begun. I was so much more settled than most of the other people I knew, yet my commitments seemed to have dwindled rather than increased.

My fellow students worried about money and pregnancy and the constant irritation of intimacy in ugly surroundings. My artist friends were old enough not to have outgrown those concerns but to simplify the last of them to the constant irritation of intimacy anywhere.

I didn't have to keep late hours to get my work done, and Rocket encouraged me to take long walks on the beach, which have always been one of my greatest pleasures. With her protective company I was also free to explore the university grant-land bush, trails intersecting for miles through scrub forest edged with berries and wild flowers. At home Maud's antics often made me laugh aloud, and her warmth in my lap as I sat reading was a simple comfort.

After Oscar, I didn't encourage already attached men to come to call without their wives or girlfriends. I deflected any domestic complaints offered over public coffee at the university or a glass of wine at an opening. I did sometimes listen to their wives as an antidote to my envy. Very few of them seemed content with their lives. In those old days I thought, though never said, that they should be. I was surprised at how many of them envied me.

"You're the only one of us the men ever listen to," one wife observed, a woman both brighter and more committed to her own mind than I was, but she was delayed in her studies by two small children and her husband's academic needs.

The men did listen to me for the simple reason that I asked good questions. Their wives wanted equal time for giving answers. Even quiet men can't tolerate that; they stop listening.

Men married to artistic rather than academic women fared little better. To the complaint that time at home was eaten up with everyone else's needs, husbands were apt to shout, "God, if I had some time at home, I'd have a poem to show for it!" This was before the time that men did stay home, even the best of them, more than once a week. Though some did laundromat duty and food shopping, they thought of these tasks as interim measures until they could make enough money not to feel humble in their expectations of service. Yet their wives also looked forward to a time when life would be made more tolerable by money.

Only one out of all those graduate-school marriages survives into the eighties. Among male artists and their wives, the odds are better (or worse, of course, depending on one's point of view). I speculate that wives of artists don't expect life to get better, early on resign themselves to or embrace a role of cherishing genius without rationalization. My mother lived that way with my father, not

43

expecting diamonds or a plumber either.

"If only men *were* superior," wailed one young wife, "it would make life so much easier."

For all their difficulties, for their envy of my freedom and serenity, I knew those women also pitied me, particularly on those occasions when I needed an escort, the more for their remembering the years of Wilson. I tried not to feel sorry for myself. I knew the Oscars of this world are worse than nothing. About the Wilsons of this world I wasn't entirely sure.

As a young woman of the eighties I might not have waited until I was 30 to consider what my own sexual tastes actually were. Perhaps I was backwards even for my own generation. I didn't give friends the opportunity to tell me so. Lee Fair was the first person, aside from my mother, in whom I ever confided. The impulse took me by surprise, for she was not only younger than I but one of my students.

Like Wilson, Lee had published a book of poems in her early twenties. Unlike him, she had then married and had a child, a choice no wiser for her than it would have been for him. Yet she defended what she had done on the grounds that motherhood is central to the female vision. No woman without that experience could have very much to say. She was too fiercely vulnerable for me to point out how few of our well-known women writers had children. The Brontës, Jane Austen, George Eliot, Emily Dickinson, Willa Cather, Gertrude Stein were all childless.

I had assumed rather than thought about children myself. I was not particularly interested in those belonging to my friends, but I did not read that as a dislike of children. Mine would be well brought up as I had been.

Lee's child, Carol, was both remarkably quiet and watchful compared to other five-year-olds I had known. I did not actively dislike her, but I was unnerved by the critical appraisal in her gaze. Any time she was due to arrive with her mother, I took as much care about my appearance as I would for a lover.

She asked odd questions, too, like, "Were you a sad little girl?" She was attracted to sorrow, as Wilson had been. She told me, "My daddy didn't die. He just went away."

Some of my childhood books were still on the shelves, and I found some of my old dolls, stuffed animals and games in the cupboard with the neglected Christmas ornaments. As Carol became accustomed to the place, she spent less time suspiciously staring, though she went on asking questions.

"Did you always play by yourself?"

"A lot of the time," I said. "I liked to. I liked to play in the garden."

Sometimes I stood by the window watching her climb among the rocks as I had done, and I supposed my mother often watched me when I was unaware of it. Then Carol would turn, look up and wave. I waved back and turned away, not wanting to seem to spy.

"You should have a child," Lee said. "Why don't you have one?"

"I manage better with animals," I replied, wondering for how many years I'd used self deprecation as a way to defend myself against personal questions.

"You mother your students."

"Do I mother you? You don't seem to me that much younger than I am."

"I'm not," Lee said. "And at the rate I'm going, I'll be twenty years older than you are by the time I finish my MA."

Lee's face was dark and strained, and there was already a lot of grey in her mane of black hair. She was always exhausted, working as a cocktail waitress on weekends, studying late into week nights, finding time for Carol.

"I don't have your stamina," I said.

"I don't have it either. I just don't have any choice… now."

Like so many other women I knew, Lee made me feel guilty, but the others all had men to stand between them and any altruism I felt. Lee was alone, and I did want to do things for her to make her life easier.

"Don't offer to do things for me," she warned, "because I'll let you."

"Is there anything immoral about doing your laundry here while you have a meal rather than down at the laundromat?"

"Not yet," Lee said.

Her guardedness, her fear of dependence, made me at first more careful of her feelings than I would otherwise have been and perhaps less aware of my own.

One afternoon, when I offered to pick Carol up at kindergarten to give Lee an extra hour at the library, she said, "Don't get indispensable."

"Oh, sometimes you seem to me as impossible as a man," I said in sudden irritation.

"Sometimes you seem as insensitive as one," she retorted.

That exchange, as I thought about it, seemed to me basically funny.

"Does neither of us like men very much?" I asked her over coffee, after Carol had been settled in my study with some books.

"I don't have anything against them as long as they leave me me alone," Lee said.

"You don't want to remarry ever?"

"No," she said. "Why do I seem to you impossible?"

"You don't. It's only that I don't expect to have to be as careful with you as…"

"With a man?"

"The men I've cared about anyway."

Then for the first time I tried to describe my years with Wilson to the final distress of having destroyed whatever it was between us by one fatal question. I talked about Oscar, too, the rigid, the controlling structures men made in which there was never simply room to be.

"Why did you choose men who didn't want you?" Lee asked.

"I wasn't aware...with Wilson anyway...that I had," I answered, but, as I saw the doubt in her expression, I supposed I wasn't telling the truth. "I don't know." "Do you really not know now either that you're choosing a woman who does want you?" Lee asked quietly, and, when I did not respond, she said, "Is that to be my fatal question?"

"It mustn't be," I finally managed to say.

"You may not be able to help that," Lee said, and then she called Carol to her and went home.

Again I was faced with my peculiar blindness to my own motives. For months I had been courting Lee in the ways traditional to a lover, rerouting myself on campus on the off chance of meeting her, stupidly disappointed when a similar head of hair revealed a much older and less appealing face. I had bought her small presents, even flowers, and taken her to restaurants and the theatre. I had taken advantage of a convention of physical affection between women to take her arm as we walked along together, to hug and even sometimes kiss her.

When Lee warned me off, there was always also an invitation in it as there had never been with Wilson, and my impatience with her caution was my desire to set no limits on my love, to let it open and flower as it would, at last.

I had never been able to tolerate Oscar's charge that Wilson was a homosexual. It was with perverse relief that

I could now exonerate him with my own sexuality, at least the possibility of it.

If I were, in fact, a lesbian, there did not have to be any limits set with Lee, who by now was no longer my student. I might even propose that she move in with me. Who could criticize such an arrangement, one woman helping another? Carol. Well, Carol could be my child, too. I had already begun to give her my childhood. Lee could give up her hideous job, even finally have time to write again. She could have my study. I did most of my work at the university anyway. And Carol could have my old room, which I now used as a guest-room.

So I sat happily rearranging the uses of the furniture without a single moral or emotional apprehension.

When I saw Lee the next day, I embraced her joyfully. Then I looked into her uncertain face and said, "Don't you see? It makes everything so much easier."

Lee laughed in disbelief.

"Tonight you won't have to wake Carol and take her home."

I felt neither shy nor frightened. Lee and I had been casually naked together in the changing-room at the pool. I already knew a delight in the shape of her breasts, the curve of her back, the length of her thighs. And I knew how tender and sure her hands were, tending her child. I also knew she wanted me and had wanted me for a long time.

When we finally lay together in absolute intimacy, all my sexual bewilderment and constraint left me. I understood my power because I could feel it in a singing heat to be fed to a roaring. I was hardly aware of Rocket's one howl, which soon faded into resignation.

"Rocket, you beast," Lee said to the dog in the morning, fondling her ears. "Did you have to make a public announcement?"

Carol said, "I had a funny dream, that I could float...in the air."

I was having the same sensation awake, a combination of euphoria and lack of sleep.

For Lee our love-making did not clear away all the obstacles. When I proposed that she give her landlord notice and move in with me, she wanted to know if I'd really thought about living not only with her but with Carol.

"She's not always an easy child."

"It isn't as if I didn't know her. Carol and I like each other."

"But you'll have to love her," Lee said.

"I do," I protested. "Why don't we ask her if she'd like it?"

"And if she says no?"

I realized I was not prepared to put my fate quite so simply at the whim of a five-year-old child.

Lee was embarrassed when I talked about money.

"You don't create a problem," I tried to explain. "You solve one."

With Lee and Carol to support there was a practical reason for me to take my academic career seriously, accept a full-time appointment the following term and have a real use for my salary. Lee could go on with her MA or not. Maybe it would be better for her to stay home, write and have more time for Carol.

"Even men resent dependents. Wouldn't you?" Lee asked.

"Why should I? You're the point of my life."

For a month Lee and Carol spent three or four nights a week with me, and we all grew increasingly tired and strained. Carol began to have unsympathetic dreams, woke needing her mother's attention.

One night I heard her say to Lee, "You smell funny."

After that Lee left a basin of water on my dresser and

washed her face and hands quickly before going to Carol. I did not quote, "Will these hands ne'er be clean?"

One morning after a particulary unsettled night, Lee said, "It isn't going to work. Carol just can't handle it."

"She simply can't handle living in two different places. Half the time she doesn't know where she is when she wakes up. If you moved in, she'd be able to settle down."

"Why don't you ever go in to her?" Lee asked.

"Well, I will from now on. It didn't occur to me," I admitted.

Of course, when I did, Carol bellowed, "I want my mother."

We decided that I should keep Carol on my own over the weekend when she saw very little of her mother anyway. It would also give Lee a chance to get the rest she badly needed. It worked because I devoted myself to Carol. I took her to the zoo. We went to a toy shop and bought new books and some doll furniture, which we set up together in her room. I fixed her her favourite macaroni and cheese, and then read to her.

The effect of such attention backfired when Lee came home. Carol simply became as demanding of me as she was of her mother, behaving very like Rocket in her attempts to keep between us, making herself the centre of attention even at the price of our irritation. Again Lee's solution was to move out, mine for them to move in, and Carol was now on my side.

Lee did not so much change her mind as give in. All in one day, she gave her notice, quit her job and dropped out of university. Then all the nervous energy that had kept her going through her impossible schedule drained from her, and she slept like a patient after major surgery.

For several weeks, I got up if Carol called in the night, got up in the morning to get her off to kindergarten and myself to UBC, collected her and brought her home to

Lee who increasingly often had not bothered to dress. I did the shopping, the cooking, the laundry, the cleaning, exercised the dog, mowed the lawn, electric with energy to be all things for Lee, provider, mother, lover, for Lee was filled with sleepy gratitude and sexual sweetness.

"Are you sick, Mommy?" Carol finally asked her.

"I suppose so," I heard Lee reply.

"Are you going to get well?"

"I suppose so," she said again, but the listlessness in her voice suddenly alarmed me.

"Are you all right?" I asked her later that night. "Are you getting rested?"

She only murmured and kissed me.

Early in the morning she was restless, got up, went to the bathroom, came back into the bedroom and stood by the window.

"Are you all right?" I asked again.

For answer she came back to bed and held me in her arms.

When I woke again, her breathing was unnaturally heavy. I tried to wake her and couldn't. The empty bottle of pills was in the bathroom for me to find. I phoned the doctor who phoned an ambulance.

When Lee had recovered enough to talk, she said, "I should have told you. I was trying to find someone to love Carol..."

"But how could you not want to live?" I asked. "We've been so happy."

She turned her face away from me and closed her eyes.

Hysterical crying or giggling are the luxuries of a woman who lives alone. I had Carol to take care of, comfort, reassure. When she had gone to sleep, I hardly had time to note my own exhaustion before I was asleep myself.

When I woke to the new, requiring day and tried to

think about Lee, I could not. I moved automatically through my appointments until lunch-time when I could spend a few minutes with her at the hospital.

"No Visitors" was posted on her shut door.

I went to find a nurse.

The nurse took me to a waiting-room. "Her mother's here. She's been trying to reach you."

"Her mother?"

I did know Lee had a mother and a father. She spoke of them very little, as little as she spoke of her ex-husband or anything else about her past. She came from Winnipeg and said that even the name of the city made her teeth hurt.

A woman with pure white hair and eyes even more exhausted than Lee's came into the room.

"Dulce?"

"Yes," I said.

"I must thank you for being so kind to Lee and Carol through this distressing time."

Kind? I could not imagine what Lee had told her mother.

"I'm making arrangements to take them back to Winnipeg with me tomorrow. Would it be convenient if I came and packed their things tonight?"

"Is that what Lee wants to do?"

"I'm afraid she doesn't have much choice. She can't simply be a burden to strangers."

"She's been no burden," I protested. "She was simply terribly tired..."

"Perhaps she hasn't told you," her mother said. "She has a history of...this."

"But Carol has just really settled in and started to feel at home."

"She hasn't had an easy life," Lee's mother said.

It wasn't exactly lack of sympathy for her own daughter

that she expressed in concern for Carol; she seemed simply saddened and resigned.

"If Lee wanted to come home to me, I'd..." I began.

"I'm so sorry. She doesn't want to see you. I'm sure she's...well...ashamed of all the trouble she's caused."

When I picked up Carol that afternoon, I looked at her soft dark cap of hair, her watchful dark eyes and could no more bear the thought of losing her than of losing Lee. What craziness was it in Lee to have thought I would be allowed Carol?

"Your grandmother's here," I said. "She's going to take you and your mother home to Winnipeg until she's better."

"Then do we get to come back here to be with you?"

"I honestly don't know. I hope so."

Carol was quiet then until we got home. She came with me, as was now her habit, to walk Rocket, who did not take her customary long circlings in the bush but stayed with us, bumping clumsily and persistently against us on the narrow path.

Over dinner Carol said, "Mommy said you'd take care of me if anything happened to her."

"She's going to be fine."

"You should make her go to school. Even kids have to go to school."

"She was only having a rest."

"That's when she always gets sick."

First her mother and now her child were tattling on Lee, for whom I felt a pointless, painful loyalty.

"Can I take my doll furniture?"

The next day there was no trace left of either Lee or Carol. I did not even think to ask for their Winnipeg address. Lee had taken my life, if not her own, in a way that I had never meant to give her.

Though it has often seemed obvious to me that troubled friends are in need of psychiatric attention, I have never known what I would say to one about myself, except perhaps that I have too often been mistaken and don't seem able to learn from life as I believe I sometimes do from paintings and poems, even occasionally from a novel.

Lee Fair wrote a novel, part of which is based on or takes off from those brief passionate months we spent together. It is always difficult to know, even when one is not personally involved, how much feeling and judgment really reflect on the raw material of life. Perhaps I would more easily and resignedly accept the portrait of me in it as Lee's real view of me if she hadn't also dedicated the book to me. Am I a muse or a villain? For the artist there may be no clear distinction. My name as a character is Swete, and I am very like the other preying lesbians about whom I compulsively read for several years after Lee left me. Swete seduces the main character and robs her of her child's affection, then of her financial independence and finally of her will to study and write until finally her only way to regain her own life is to take it. The main character recovers to marry her psychiatrist, as Lee also did, though she divorced him not long after the book was published.

Lee is now one of Canada's best known lesbians, that first novel something of an embarrassment to her. To her credit, she uses it as an example of how we have been raised to trash each other and seek our salvation in men. Carol's two sons keep Lee from the extremes of separatism. Lee and I exchange Christmas cards, and we have dinner together occasionally when she is in Vancouver to give a reading or lecture. I don't ever attend them, and she has never asked for an explanation. Perhaps she remembers that I don't go to Wilson's either.

I have long since given up fantasies of nursing either

54

one of them in old age. In any case, I will sooner need that attention than either of them will whose bones are not so well acquainted with sea mists as mine are.

What I have come to understand about myself is that I am interested in art rather than artists. Those who blundered into my life under the mistaken impression that I had either something to give or be given have only threatened my pleasure in their very real accomplishments.

So many people seem to draw their nourishment directly from passion as plants take nourishment directly from the sun. I have been only badly burned by such heat. Yet the art that has been made from it has sustained me all my solitary life.

I still prefer those arts that don't require the presence of human beings: literature, painting, sculpture. Films are less threatening to me than live theatre, and I prefer my music canned.

After Lee, I encouraged neither men nor women in any sort of intimacy; yet I have gone on being for one artist or another a symbol until I've become something of a legend myself. It is not really respectable, in western Canada, anyway, for a poet to pass 30 without having written a poem to me. I have been muse, witch, preying lesbian. I have also been devouring mother, whore, Diana, spirit of Vancouver, daughter of the tides.

In a sense my life has been lived for me in the imaginations of other people, and there is nothing dangerous about that if I don't try to participate, for in that way disaster lies. My real companions, in my imagination, are my counterparts throughout history and the world who, whatever names they are given, are women very like myself, who holds the shell of a poem to her ear and hears the mighty sea at a safe and sorrowing distance.

Man in the Black Magic Box

Robert G. Sherrin

You Are standing in Place du Canada.

You're in front of a bus with the word DUBONNET on its side.

Your *Herald Tribune* is folded on a table in the Hotel Alma.

There are ads for everything. For men who are lonely and for men who want to be alone. Ads for cheap cars, propane tanks still wedged in the trunks, little signs in German stapled to the backs of the seats. There are ads for clubs where men dress as women and ads for men who will give you twice the going rate for your Canadian dollars. They come with briefcases full of francs and do transactions in the park, or in your hotel room, or in the café where you drink *bière d'Alsace* and watch people drift away from you.

There are ads for everything in Paris in 1953.

There's a photograph in the *Ottawa Citizen* that year of a young girl picking the first daffodils of spring. And there are photos in the Black Magic box of a man who wears a long tweed coat, hands always thrust into the pockets. He squints forever into the sun: in front of a metro sign that says PIGALLE, or a restaurant called Doucets, or a gallery poster for Ellen Logeais. The *Citizen* is folded on a kitchen table above the Jamaica Confectionery. On the front page, the girl bends over to pick daffodils, blond hair held by two barrettes. She's seven years old. At home, above the Jamaica Confectionery, she has postcards stuck to the fridge.

Perspective du Paris
photo by Guy

She goes to school in the daytime. Classmates ask about her brother. She says he is so young, still messes his bum, has to be told when to use the toilet. She talks about the tall woman who sleeps in the back room and buys poor meat at the Jamaica Confectionery, who always leans over the Moffat range or closes the door of the bathroom to be alone. The girl smiles as she peels back the bread to remove the lettuce from her sandwich and thinks of the tall woman who sleeps alone in the big bed, who often wakes her in the early morning to take her to the couch and wrap them in a blanket to watch the sun rise over the chainlink fence across the street. The blond girl turns in her lunch-room seat and exchanges a fig newton for a lemon tart with the boy behind her.

The clock says 12.19.

The calendar says Friday the seventeenth, 1953.

She turns back to the bread and presses the two pieces more firmly together, sees again her mother emerge from the back room, meringue-coloured robe loosely knotted at the waist, blond hair falling in ropes halfway down her back, hand to mouth, bare feet shuffling to the bathroom. The boy cries in his crib, the old man unlocks the downstairs door and drags in metal cases of bottled milk. She imagines the tall woman hunched over the toilet and turns away, shakes her head to clear it of the chainlink fence and the echoing from the bathroom. She squeezes the bread till her thumb and forefinger meet. Then she sets the sandwich aside, quietly folds her hands and stares at the photo above the blackboard: a colour print of the Queen and her bonny prince, forever together, one in robes of purple, the other in red sash and silver sword.

You hear the taxis go by, tires hissing in the springtime. If you had more money, you'd go to Au Printemps for breakfast. Take the escalator. Up past men's suits, women's lingerie, hers always in pale pink or turquoise. Up past the bed linen, yours now white, but not long ago, a swirl of flowers that seemed to entangle you both. Up past the appliances, the old Moffat sweet with leakage, your little coffee-maker on the table in the Alma, *Herald Tribune* in a ball beside it. Up past the furniture, all wicker this year, your stick chair in the hotel unsteady on its feet, the studio couch in Ottawa a soft barge on which you'd lie and smoke cigarettes rolled in Vogue papers. She'd leave half an apple in the tobacco tin, liked to remove her clothes in the full, soft light of the bedroom, the vanity mirror tilted so she could watch you watch her. Up till you find yourself—shocked at your ability to make it there—in the round, open foliage of the restaurant. The top of Au Printemps is covered in umbrellas of stained glass, the smell of *café au lait* and *croissant avec beurre* drawing you to a table for two under a palm. Just the way you'd have done it if she were there and you wanted to tell her something without opening your mouth.

Instead, you roll in the big bed, half of it smooth as tile, reach for the lamp and douse the light, fall back to drape your arms over your face and listen to the woman downstairs calling to her daughter. Across the street, the boucher slides the steel jalousies from his storefront, pigeons rattle on the roof, klaxons wail on Rue Sommerard. The bedsprings grunt as you methodically pound your feet into the mattress and try to sleep the day away.

The blond girl walks up Rideau to the Chateau Laurier and enters the main lobby. She used to hear stories from the tall woman and the man in the Black Magic box about the day they arrived in their nation's capital and could not find a room. They'd pulled in at the Lord Elgin, the slope-backed Dodge left idling in the drive, and approached the desk in their soiled car coats, toques stuffed into pockets, and asked for a room. The clerk eyed them, smiled and requested their reservations. They had none. She recalled the way her father's feet tapped one against the other as he leaned into the counter and spoke in lowered tones about the drive from the Yukon in the middle of winter, his six-year-old daughter needing a decent bed. She'd noticed how he pressed his thighs against the desk as if he were trying to dance with the clerk. She'd taken the rough cotton of his pants in her hands and twisted it. Even at the age of six she knew what the answer would be. So they'd turned the Dodge into the traffic, coasting to a halt in front of the Chateau and walked in, stood tightly together in the lobby, suddenly joined by fear and loneliness into a single organism. It was her mother who moved first. She touched her husband on the sleeve and edged away, picked up speed, walked crisply to the desk, shook her head a few times, then glanced back to smile. A bellhop responded to the clerk and asked them for the keys to the Dodge, would return with their luggage and show them to their room.

Now she was in the lobby by herself. She stared at the brightly tiled ceiling, felt the movement of people about her, the rustle of their clothes, the fast clip of their voices, the back-beat of feet advancing and retreating over the carpet and marble. She approached the desk and the clerk looked down at her. Could he help? Was cinnamon toast still served in the restaurant? Yes. Could she please sit there, by herself, and order some? Yes. She smiled. Was she a guest of the hotel? She shook her head. The clerk signalled for a boy and a bellhop in a pillbox hat appeared and was asked to show her to the dining-saloon and see that she received what she wanted.

I can pay.

She smiled again.

The clerk nodded. Yes. We all can.

The bellhop extended his hand, but she lefts hers in her pocket and followed him over the carpet, down the corridor. The news-stand had the last three editions of the *Citizen* prominently displayed. On the front pages are shots of the prime minister, a man jumping from a window and her with daffodils in her hand.

She was given a deuce with a linen cloth. She folded her gloves on the table and asked for cinnamon toast.

Mother would be walking home from the Sears catalogue office. Her brother would be asleep in another suite over the Jamaica Confectionery. Their neighbour would be humming songs that jumped back and forth like people dancing. And her father would be standing in front of a big word in another city.

The jalousies are made of wood and sometimes they don't work. When it rains, the slats swell and if you've been long in the cafés or have spent the day and night walking, or taking photos, or looking for the men with the brief-cases full of francs, you'll return to the Alma to find that the blinds can't be lowered. You'll sit at the table, with the *Trib* and scan the personals.

HAPPY BIRTHDAY my little black
nigger. Much love, R.

You've seen the ad at least ten times. What does it mean? There's never been a response. Who places it? Why pay for it? What love have they lost, hope to gain, to keep unchanged?
Chère amie.
At one time there were letters every third or fourth day. You read them all, carefully refolded the blue onionskins and slid them back into the envelopes that said PAR AVION and gave a return address that you didn't know. You'd lost that town. Was it near the river? Near the Supreme Court? Was she working for a judge who gave her legal advice? Would there be communiqués from lawyers, or would it be letter after letter detailing her every day, disassembling her activities and placing them before you like struck pets brought in from the roadway to die? You shrugged. You yawned. You put the letters in a Salamander box and pushed it under the bed. You sent postcards in reply.
Je pense
Vous pensez
Nous pensons
Pictures of the Tour d'Eiffel, L'Arc, Notre Dame,

photo by Guy, purchased cheaply in Metro stations: Mutualité-Maubert, Pyramides, Gare du Nord. You put large stamps on them. Say nothing as boldly as possible. Give no indication of returning. Say nothing of your health, money, love or desires. Drop the images, bits of architecture only, into a pillar box and walk from the Bureau de Poste back to the Alma and lower the jalousies.

Then the letters stopped.

You thought the mails had slowed down. You thought that Mme. Wegren was holding them because you hadn't paid for the last change of linen. You thought the postman was reading them. They'd found out about your wife and daughter and your little son. They sneered at your hasty talk of research and an office on the other side of the river. They no longer thought you pensive. They thought you a thief, stealing time and affection from others. Why would you come to a place like Paris, city of love?

But no.

The letters just stopped.

Tant pis.

You slept all day. You had dreams of the blond girl who used to dash ahead of the two of you then come running back, arms wide like the wings of a plane, swoop under your joined hands and pivot to buzz you again. You dreamed of the little house near the canal. You saw the two small bedrooms and the living-room with the fireplace and the hardwood floors. You smelled the bacon and the cabbage and the rice. You heard the man you worked for tell you things over the phone. You recalled the woman in the office who asked you for help with her estate taxes and wore red-and-blue and walked ahead and opened her door for you.

It wasn't love. But it was enough. She left for the West Coast with her dead husband's money.

The walks stopped. You dreamed the chair in the back

yard. While the tall blond woman made food or washed her hair or sat naked in front of the vanity and watched her belly grow, you were in the yard, feeling suddenly a prisoner, watched the grass get longer and the apples drop to the ground and the peas get run over by weeds. You didn't understand why you wanted to be alone. Then you heard yourself say it aloud: I have to get out.

Why?

Parce que.

Pourquoi?

Because.

There were no reasons given. The letters just stopped. And then the dreams stopped. They you stayed in bed all day and only thought about going out. Your money might last another four months.

I have to get out.

Her face turning from the mirror to look at you. Her back long and arched. Her stomach hard and round. Her breasts swollen and heavy, a weight you remember as she pressed against you then pulled herself to her knees and took your hand and put it where she wanted it.

I have to get out.

Of what?

Her face turning from the vanity mirror. Her back long and arched. Her stomach hard and round. Her hands at the straps on her shoulders, her breasts loose and swollen. Her hair swinging in the soft light of the bedroom, the mirror tilted so she could watch you watch her. But now she had turned.

I have to get out.

Of what?

Of this.

And your hand sweeping the air, indicating room, house, job, relationship. As if you were making a geographical statement, not admitting you'd fallen out of

love.
Combien?
Beaucoup.
Combien exactement?
Tous ce que vous avez.

The tall woman sleeps alone in a wide bed. At one time she'd spread one of his shirts on the pillow next to her. Then she switched sides, preferring to rest on his, preferring to cry or stare at the light on the table until her eyes fell only because she couldn't keep them raised. Took pills that the doctor prescribed. Slept deeply when she took them but felt unrested in the morning. Sometimes she saw his face in her sleep. Eventually she had to struggle to bring his features to mind.

The tall woman tends to her children. She buys jars of peanut butter, lettuce and chicken-noodle soup at the Jamaica Confectionery. She fills the suite with the smells of burned liver-and-onions. She sits in the window and watches the chainlink fence across the street. It cuts the world into tiny squares. She seems to occupy none of them. The radio talks of Korea and the need for commitment in the world of today.

She laughs.

The world of today.

She surveys her landscape. The studio couch, the blanket on it. The little boy crawls now and has to be watched all the time. Her daughter goes to school and comes home as late as she can, says as little as possible, tapes her father's postcards to the fridge, rescues the Black Magic box from the garbage and keeps it under her bed. The tall woman shakes her head. She runs a hand through her hair and curls her feet under herself.

At one time she liked the feel of him, the way his hand could move slowly yet quicken the pace of sensation.

64

She'd liked the way he could find a word for anything, how he chattered over the table, bathed their daughter, told her nonsense till she fell asleep. She'd liked the way he watched her disrobe, the way he sat on the bed, back against the wall, legs apart, hands behind his head, sometimes talking to her in a soft voice, sometimes watching her slow movements then closing his eyes, waiting for her to surprise him.

Now she had come to like the feel of herself, the ability to stretch a little more each day across the wide bed. She didn't like the smell of liver or pork, nor the perpetual darkness of her room. She didn't like the cold porcelain of the toilet bowl under her arms or the way the fridge whined or the way the gas smelled. She didn't like that she and her daughter didn't talk much, or seemed to speak through layers of cloud, voices barely audible, no hellos or goodbyes. But she did like the fact that she wrote no more letters. She liked the fact that she could listen to her own silence and not want to fill it with mourning. She liked the way her hands rested on her thighs and didn't shake or reach for the Players Plain.

Springtime.

There's a newspaper photo tacked to the wall. Her daughter posing over a bed of daffodils. Her son sleeps in the suite across the hall and she has another twenty minutes before she is due to collect him and drop the dollar bill into Marianne's pink, well-lined hand.

She gets the Black Magic box and sits back down. There he is. In front of the equine statue at Longchamps. There he is in front of a plane in the Yukon. There he is in front of a Metro stop.

There he is. there he is there he is.

There he isn't.

She lays the photos out, like a deck of face cards. She arranges them in suits of time then moves them one over another, profile over face over squint over scowl, a hand of solitaire almost two years in the playing. He merges into the paper and the chemicals and becomes a silent thing. A stack of old images, a collage of histories, closely defined in black-and-white but meaningless in his absence, his disappearance, his getting out.

I'll be gone till I get back.

Come back. Please.

And she laughs softly.

All the letters in the PAR AVION envelopes. All the silent meals of cabbage rolls, three plates, she eating two servings just to preserve the memory, looking up, tears rolling, a fork in each hand, to see her daughter staring at her then slowly rising to hide in her room. Then the boy arrived and his cries and the need to find smaller, less expensive accommodation. Jamaica Confectionery. Half the furniture gone.

She dumps him back in his box. She watches him watch her as she lowers the lid and rises to fetch her son.

The blond girl left the Chateau and walked back along the river. She recalled running along this promenade, arms akimbo, sailing like an airship, sweeping past the tall woman and the man with the rough cotton pants. She felt again the plucking of the wind, the slap of the pavement and the smell of wet grass. She remembered the joined hands, the way the sun caught the gold on the fingers, flashing a semaphore at her. Just like she learned in Brownies.

This code cannot be broken.

Ah, but it has been.

She thrust her hands deeper into her pockets. The cinnamon toast had been served hot. At the end of her tiny meal, the waiter had brought a silver bowl of water and, unlike the first time in that dining-saloon, she hadn't hoisted it to her mouth to drink. This time she'd lowered her fingers one by one then wiped them on the napkin. She'd left her 40¢ on the table and walked out of the carpets and cold marble into the sun and a warm breeze.

It was 1953.

She was nine years old.

Her brother was fourteen months.

Her mother was 31.

Her father lived in a Black Magic box.

She knew he would stay there.

She followed the river until the road curved toward the Jamaica Confectionery. She climbed the narrow staircase and opened the chipped white door. The radio was playing something with lots of horns. Her brother was sitting on the floor pointing at her.

She grinned back at him and turned down the hall to drop her coat on her bed. She glanced into the back bedroom. Then she stepped inside. The blinds were raised. The bed was made. The sheet had been taken from the vanity mirror.

She could not remember sunlight in this room.

She turned to see the tall woman in the doorway. They stared at each other like children meeting for the first time. Her mother wore an apron. Her hair was brushed out and fell over her shoulders like the flaps of a blond tent. She tossed her head and smiled at her daughter. Then she waved. Slowly the blond girl waved back.

"Hi there," her mother said.

"Hi."

They watched one another for a moment. The room seemed suddenly larger. Her mother took her by the shoulders, hands smelling of fresh fruit.

"Hungry?"

"Yes."

"Good. So am I."

You sit at a table in the Hotel Alma. You place the PAR AVION envelopes, one by one, in the Salamander shoebox and tie a string around it. You fold the *Trib* and place it beside the coffee-maker. You take your coat and drape it over your arm.

The street is slick with sunshine. You have no dark glasses. You squint and push into the crowds, stopping at your café where one-armed Sidney plays trumpet. You order a *bière d'Alsace*.

Combien?

Un, soixante quinze.

C'est tout?

Oui.

Pourquoi?

Parce que.

You go to the agency with the box of letters under your arm. There, you catch the eye of the clerk and she comes to help you. You ask a question. She consults the fare schedule.

Onze mille cinq cent quarante.

C'est vrai?

C'est vrai.

You turn away and lean against the counter and tap your feet together. You touch your face. Sweat comes out. You take a deep breath. You can't seem to let it go.

You're standing in the Agence de Voyage.

You see a bus go by.

A *Herald Tribune* is folded on your table in the Hotel Alma.

The Accident

Sheldon Currie

He could still remember the hand he had when the phone rang. The seven, three, queen and five of spades, and the three of hearts turned up. Fifteen-two, fifteen-four, fifteen-six and a pair of threes for eight and the flush for twelve.

Afterwards he told people that when Christie went to answer it, he sat there and knew that the message was for him, and he knew what it was. He looked at the four spades and said to himself: I hope he's not killed.

His friend Archie, on his right at the square dining-room table, was humming the Kyrie Eleison. Any other time, Christie, Archie's mother, when she came back would say: "Archie, for God's sake stop that mournful noise," but this time, Ian knew, she would not. Across the table Archie's father drummed his fingers on the table and said, "You fellahs better have good pegging cards, if you don't want to be skunked." Another time Ian would have said. "You said it partner." But this time he stared at his spades.

There was no telephone in his own house and the ring always sounded to him like an explosion, and every time he heard it, he expected it would bring news of his father's death. When he heard Christie's voice diminish, and say to the telephone, "Ian's here now, mumble mumble mumble," he thought, "I knew it. I knew it when it rang."

"There's an accident in 25," Christie said. She put her hand on Ian's shoulder. He stared at his spades and waited. "Two men are killed and two men are hurt."

"My father is one of the four?"

"Yes."

"Are they up?"

"Mrs. McLeod it was that called. She didn't know if they were up yet or not."

"Okay. I better go."

"You want me to drive you," Archie said.

"No. I'll run home. My cousin is visiting. Her husband will take me out."

"Good luck," Christie said.

"Thanks," he said, and ran off in the dark.

There was a good chance his mother didn't know yet. Someone would have to call a neighbour. The neighbour would have to run over. They'd want to wait until they had definite news. He started to run faster. He was glad they didn't have a telephone. What a way to find out, especially if Johnny and Daisy were gone. If they were gone he'd have to get someone else to drive him. He slowed down to a walk. He didn't have far to go but it was pitch black. The road was rocky. He had been playing cards at his friends the MacNeils, who lived across the highway in the newest of the co-op housing groups. Once across the highway there were lights and the road was graded and he started running, but he was soon near his driveway, the first one, in the oldest of the co-op housing groups. He walked the short driveway slowly, so he wouldn't be huffing and puffing going into the house.

His mother stood at the stove when he opened the door; in one hand she held the lifter with the cover hooked onto it, in the other hand she held the poker and was thrusting it into the burning coal.

"Well, you're back," she said. "Want a cup of tea? I'm just about to put some on."

"You didn't hear the news?"

"News. What news? Oh my God. Your father."

"They called MacNeils. I came right up."

"He's dead?"

"I don't think so."

"I think he's dead."

"There were four in it. Two are dead. But two are just hurt. I think Dad's just hurt."

"Oh God. I can't believe it."

"I better go and find out," he said. Johnny came out and offered to take him in his truck.

"Thanks," Ian said.

"Where'll we go?" Johnny said. "The pit or the hospital?"

"Better go to the pit first. They mightn't have them up yet. And even so we don't know what hospital. If they were bad off they might just go to the closest."

Ian expected a big crowd to be milling around the pit

head, but there was nobody. It had started to drizzle. Johnny stopped the truck in the middle of the yard near the wash-house. The lights on the poles seemed able to light up only themselves; the buildings were soft shadows and in the wet dark seemed larger than they were. The door of the wash-house opened and let out a thick slice of light and a man with a lunch can under his arm. The door slammed shut. The man diminished to a shadow and disappeared around the corner. "We might as well go in there," Ian said.

Ian pulled open the door and stepped in. The room was steamy and crowded. A few men were still in their pit clothes, a few in their street clothes. Most were naked, half of them blackfaced with coal dust, the other half had finished showering and were pulling their street clothes down on the ropes and pulleys that kept them near the roofbeams while the men were in the pit. Ian wound his way through the crowd of men until he found a familiar face. "What happened, Frankie, where's Dad?"

"He's at St. Joseph's. They just left."

"We didn't pass them."

"They probably went the Sydney road way. You must of come through Rabbittown."

"Is he all right?"

"I don't know. He's hurt pretty bad. Likely he'll be all right. He was hunched down next to the machine. He got squeezed in the wedge but I think it saved him. Peter got killed."

"Peter?"

"Peter your cousin. He just started workin' with your father."

"Oh God."

"Roddie got killed."

"MacEachern?"

"Yeah. And Joe got hurt, don't know how bad. They

took him off in the same truck with your father. They had the priest out for the other two. I heard him say St. Joseph's."

"Okay, I better get down there."

"Tell your father I'll be down later."

Inside the hospital front door the receptionist told him "down them steps straight ahead, right at the bottom is the room." At the bottom step he saw the family doctor come out a doorway facing the stair.

"How is he?"

"Touch and go," he said, and fled down the hall. "So far so good," he said over his shoulder and went through a doorway.

Ian went in. There was nothing in it but his father on his back, knees up, and a bed with steel legs and big rubber wheels. He was just as they pulled him out. The right leg of his pants was ripped to the knee. A gash like a long mouth full of blood and coal dust ran from knee to ankle. The ankle looked like a bone sticking out of a roast. The right arm of his shirt was off. The arm was black where it wasn't blue. His hands were on his belly palms down, the tips of his middle fingers touching. His face was black where it wasn't red. His hair was full of blood.

"Hello Dada," Ian said. His father moved his black middle fingers and his blue eyes.

"How bad is it?" His father beckoned him down with his black index finger. Ian put his ear down close to his father's mouth.

"The son of a whore got me by the throat," he said. "Say a prayer, eh."

"I will."

"Put your head up now. I can talk loud enough. I didn't think I could." The voice was strong but whispery and gurgly. Ian straightened up.

"Does your mother know?"

"Yes, but she doesn't know yet if you're hurt or dead."

"Tell her I'll be okay. I think I can beat the son of a whore."

"Okay, just a minute. Johnny's out there. He drove me down. I'll go tell him to go up and tell them. I'll stay here." He went to the door and found Johnny sitting on the steps.

"How is he?"

"Don't know. Hurt bad but he'll be okay I think. I'm gonna stay. Would you go and tell mother. Tell her he's gonna be okay. He'll be in for a while, but he'll be okay."

Back in the room, Ian found his father unconscious. His eyes were closed but his mouth was open, the teeth clenched and the lips pulled back in a grimace. There must be some other way a person could make a living, Ian thought. His father's eyes opened.

"You're back," he said.

"Yes."

"Was I out long?"

"No. Just a minute."

"Ian."

"Yeah."

"My feet are awful sore. Would you take off the boots?"

"Okay," Ian said and went to the foot of the bed and started to unlace the boots when he was startled by a harsh female voice.

"What are you doing?"

"Takin' off his boots."

"Who are you?"

"I'm Ian. His son."

"Oh, okay, take out the laces. But don't move the feet. I see he's unconscious again." She was only a few years older than Ian but she talked as if she owned the hospital. "I'm Sister Magdelene of the Holy Eucharist," she said,

74

and pulled the foot-long pair of scissors out of a holster at her hip and took a few snips at the air over her shoulder.

"What's wrong with him?"

"Nothing much," she said. "His back is broke. Four broken ribs. He might have a rib stickin' in a lung. His head is split, his spinal cord might be injured. Broken ankle, twisted knee plus a million cuts and bruises. My guess is he'll live. But x-rays will tell the tale. Have you got the laces out?"

"One."

"Okay, do the other," she said and she took the scissors and cut all the buttons off the shirt, then snipped it across the chest. She opened his belt, cut open his fly, snipped the pants across, then up the legs, folded everything back, slashed at both legs of his father's boxer shorts until finally everything but the shoes were in rags, hanging down from the sides of the bed and his father lay stark naked, his penis hard and sticking straight up in the air.

"See that," she said, "I told you he'd live. They're often like that after an accident," she said. "It's because they think they're going to heaven. Did you finish the laces?"

Ian stared between his fathers knees. He couldn't get his mouth going to say yes.

"Don't be embarrassed," she said, "I'm used to it. I used to be a whore, before I entered the convent. I guess that's why they put me down here." She came to the end of the bed and went to work with the scissors on the shoes. "You go to the next room," she said, "and bring in that pan of water by the sink and start washing him. Once we get him clean we can cover him up and up he goes. Go ahead now, this kind of thing is easier on you if you keep busy and keep talking so you don't get mopey."

When they finished they put him, bed and all, covered with a sheet, on the elevator. "Sister Mary'll look after him now," she said to Ian, "won't you Sister Mary?"

"Yes," Sister Mary said through the elevator door. She smiled.

"They won't let me up there," Sister Magdelene of the Holy Eucharist said. "They're scared I'll say something dirty and disgrace the order. Isn't that it Sister Mary?"

"Yes," said Sister Mary. She smiled.

"How about you stay here and help me with the other one," she said to Ian. "You might as well while you're waiting. C'mon, his two legs are broke—he might be cranky."

The other one was Joe the Pig Two MacDonald. The name he inherited from his father, also Joe MacDonald, nicknamed to distinguish him from the dozen or so other Joseph MacDonalds, most of whom had somewhat weaker distinctions such as D.P., Joe D., ABCD and so on, and because he once pronounced to his buddies, during a tea-break in the pit, one of the few general conclusions he had distilled from 40 years of living: "You know," he said, "a man had a good pig, he wouldn't be in the need of a wife."

It turned out Joe the Pig Two was not cranky. He was sore, exhausted and astonished at his good luck, having once again escaped death. His mood shifted between sorrow when he thought of his two dead buddies, and happiness when he thought of himself and Angus and their wives and all their kids.

"Watch them scissors, Maggie," he said to Sister Magdelene. "My wife'll be down to inspect and if she finds anything missing she'll be fit to be tied."

"Don't worry me b'y, it's only your legs'll be shorter. The rest of you'll be all right."

"You don't mean that. My legs."

"No no no. Just kiddin'. They won't need to cut them off."

"How is Angus makin' out?"

76

"Gone up for x-rays. I think he'll be good."

"Thank Christ. Them other two didn't have a fuckin' hope. Excuse me, Sister."

"It's okay."

"What happened, anyway, Joe?" Ian said.

"Whole goddamn roof came down on us. I heard 'er crack and jumped for the door. Got everything out but the last of my legs. Broke both, crushed a foot. Your father was hunched down by the machine. Saved him. Held up one side of the stone enough. He was crushed in there but it was enough room. Peter and Roddie were in deeper. Flattened like pancakes. Your father said that roof was no good before we started. Too late now."

"Now turn over on your belly," Sister Magdelene of the Holy Eucharist said and Joe the Pig Two turned over and she began to wash his back.

"Could I ask you a question Sister?"

"Ask away."

"Well, I got two questions," he said. "One is, how much would you charge a week to do this every day? And the other is, would you make house calls?"

"You don't shut up," she said, "I'm goin' for the scissors again. Ian would you go and change the water. I think it's makin' him worse."

The coffins at both funerals were closed. At Roddie the Log MacEachern's wake the children were all grown, the widow sedate and the wake was calm, sombre and formal. It was Ian's first Protestant funeral, and once in the little front-room where the mourners were gathered he discovered there was no kneeling bench, and since the coffin was closed, he felt silly standing there looking at its brown curved top. So he knelt anyway, thinking that no-one could object to a prayer, even a Catholic prayer. But with all the Protestant eyes arrayed around the room he couldn't bring himself to make the sign of the the cross

77

and finally in his confusion he didn't even pray; he held his hands together on his belt-buckle and studied the curlicues on the burnished brass handles of the box.

Before getting to his feet he tried to figure out where he could go next. Most times he simply said a prayer and left unless it was a wake of a close relative. But this time he felt he was here as a representative of the family, for his father who was still in the hospital, for his mother who was still reeling and for his brothers and sister who would come too but who were younger than himself and still officially children. He noticed that the regular living-room furniture had been removed and replaced by kitchen chairs and card-table chairs, which were lined around the walls. The people in them were not looking at him at all, but quietly talking or looking at their hands, knees or feet. He spotted some empty spaces and walked over and sat. The widow, Mrs. MacEachern, came and sat beside him.

"Thank you for coming, Ian," she said.

"That's okay," he said, "I'm sorry it happened." It was what his mother told him to say. "How are you feeling?"

She wore a black dress with a black belt and silver buckle, and black shoes and a bit of black hat with a black veil hanging from it over her eyes. It was the first time he had seen a veil on a grown woman. Behind the veil her eyes were quiet and blank as if concentrating intently on some unimportant distraction.

"I'm fine for now," she said. "How is your father?"

"Well, he's very sore, but they're saying he'll be okay."

"And Joseph, too, will recover?"

"Yes."

"His legs are broken?"

"Yes," Ian said.

"He'll be better soon."

"Yes."

"How long will your father be in the hospital?"

"I don't know. At least a month, I guess."

"Does he get up?"

"No, not yet."

"How is your mother?"

"She hasn't gotten over it yet. She's still not sure he's going to get better."

"Poor thing," she said. "Well, at least in the end, she'll have him back."

"Yes, that's true."

"Have you been to Peter's wake?"

"No. I'm going after."

"I was over before," she said. "Poor Gloria is taking it awful hard."

"I heard that, but I wasn't over yet."

"You can't talk to her."

"I heard she can't stop crying."

"She can't. She can't help it. She does stop sometimes, but the minute you start to talk to her, or she tries to talk to you, she starts to sob."

"They say she doesn't sleep," he said.

"She'll doze off. But she hasn't left the room to sleep or eat. She won't leave the room. She sits there and every now and again she gets up and goes over and puts her hand on the coffin. It's closed, you know, same as Roddie's. She goes back and sits. She won't leave the room."

"Yes. I heard that."

"She's young though," Mrs. MacEachern said. "She'll get over it. Next week she'll stop."

"Yes," Ian said. "She's young. She has two babies."

"Yes. Next week she'll stop," Mrs. MacEachern said. "And when she stops, then I'll start."

Ian felt he should say something reassuring, but he couldn't think of anything. He looked through the veil at her fearful eyes. "This week," she said, "I'm talking to people. I hope they don't mind."

"I'm sure no-one minds," Ian said. "Everyone knows how hard it is."

"Yes. We're all used to it. We know how hard it is. I always see you going back and forth to school. Ever since you moved up Sidney Road. But this the the first chance I had to talk to you."

"That's right," Ian said. "I still don't know many people up this way."

"Do you know my Roddie's nickname?"

"Yes."

"Do you know how he got it?"

"No. I never heard," Ian said, although he had. He wanted to hear her version.

"When the kids were little, we had a fire. We were in the company house then, up in Reserve Rows. I was right there when it happened, in the kitchen, having a cup of tea with my sister, Marie, but I don't know yet how it got started. The wall behind the stove broke into flames. It was hot, I guess. The middle of July. I was baking bread. Three of the kids were sick upstairs having a nap. The baby was in the front room. Marie ran for the fire department. This was just after they got their truck. I got all the kids out and the men came and put out the fire. The place was a mess. Water all over the kitchen. When the smoke cleared we cleaned it up and sat down to our tea again. The kids were all excited, the baby was crying. It started again. They had to come again and put it out. This time they had to rip open the wall. This time we took the kids over to Marie's. We had our tea there. An hour later there's a knock at the door and who comes in but Roddie. "Flora," he says. "What's goin' on? There's water all over the kitchen floor." Well we laughed to kill ourselves. I forgot what shift he was on. I thought he was at work. He slept through the two fires. Never even knew they happened. But I thought afterwards. He could have been burned alive and I wouldn't have known, thinking he was all the time at work. Or course when your father heard that, he said now that's what I call sleeping like a log. I felt guilty for years thinking I could have as good as killed him. Now he's dead anyway. He was an awful good man. Thank God it wasn't me that killed him. Come on to the kitchen Ian and have a cup of tea and a bite. They called him the Log ever since. Roddie the Log MacEachern."

"Thanks," Ian said. "I might have a cup."

Fortified with tea and pieces of ham, Ian walked down Sidney Road past the corner where it met Main Street to the rows of company houses in the Lorway. He didn't know the house but he kept on until he saw the wreath beside the front door. He had known Peter and he knew Gloria. They had been in the same grade together. He had walked with her the mile or so to school every day when they lived in Reserve Rows. Peter, who lived in Rabbittown, walked down the tram-car tracks and joined them every day where the tracks and Main Street came together. Ian courted her as far as there, in his indirect fashion, every day. He had to stop it there because she was Peter's girl. She knew he was courting her but he did it so she could know it and not acknowledge it. She never acknowledged it. "I'm telling you this," she said, "as if you were my brother, because I know you won't breathe a word. I'm going to marry Peter, or I'm going to be a nun."

"Gloria in excelsis Deo," he said.

"Yes," she said, "or Peter."

"What about Gloria in excelsis Ian?"

"Nope," she said. "It's God or Peter."

"I'm pulling for God," Ian said.

"Well, I'm pulling for Peter, tell you the truth," she said.

When she became pregnant, God dropped out of the competition. "I'm glad," she told Ian. "I'm not cut out for a nun, anyway. I just love Sister Immaculata and her servabo me servabo te. I'd like to be able to talk like that, but I know I'm not cut out for it. You maybe, but not me. I'll be sorry to quit though. Peter'll have to quit too. He doesn't like school a lot, but he's doing okay."

"Will you finish the year?"

"I think I will, if I don't get too big. Peter thinks he'll be hired on right away. If he is he's gonna quit."

"Will you tell Sister Immaculata?"

"I think I'll just let her find out. I wonder what she'll say?"

"I know what she'll say," Ian said.

"What?"

"She'll say passer mortuus est meae pullae."

"What does that mean?"

"It means you better get ready to do your own flying."

When Ian arrived at Peter's wake the priest and the nuns were there, all kneeling in front of chairs around the wall saying the rosary. Gloria was sitting in a corner in a stuffed chesterfield chair her mother had brought back into the front-room, hoping that its comfort would seduce her to sleep. She sat at the front edge of it, her elbows on her knees, her face in her hands. Her sobs were dry.

They were beginning the first Sorrowful Mystery, "The Agony in the Garden."

Ian knelt on the kneeling-bench in front of the coffin and looked at the brown polished wood. After he said a few prayers he saw there was no convenient place to go in the small room; people were kneeling out in the middle of the floor as well as in front of the chairs at the wall, so he stayed on the bench in front of the coffin and joined in the prayers, led by the priest. "Hail Mary, full of Grace, the Lord is with thee, blessed art thou among women and blessed is the fruit of thy womb..."

Because he couldn't see Peter's face in the coffin, his head filled with images of Peter in their common past. He and Peter hunting squirrels with their slingshots; digging a bootleg pit, thinking they would make a fortune selling coal and take a trip to Boston to see their cousins; swimming naked in the icy May water in the So'West Brook; walking out to Dominion Beach in the hot summer to dash into the icy ocean, three miles of walking with the gang and telling dirty jokes, and after swimming, sitting around the beach, talking to the girls, and trying to be mature; Peter sliding into second base and standing up in one motion, Peter scoring a goal with a backhand shot over the goalie's shoulder after he thought Peter had made the turn around the net; Peter racking up 56 points off the break to start a winning streak; playing snooker for three months with the same quarter in his pocket; he had it so long, he said, that he rubbed the king off one side and the moose off the other, so when he finally lost a game, Joe thought it was a slug and wouldn't take it, so he had to owe him for the time. Peter pulling out an unexpected pint of rum when they were taking the short-cut home after the dance, saying, "Have a sluga black death," and passing it back and forth, and throwing the empty in a high arc over the trees, and standing there, his penis gleaming in the moonlight, saying, "Have a sluga white death," and Ian saying, "No thanks, I just had an orange." And laughing.

Ian, without thinking, lifted his hands from his belt-buckle and put them on the edge of the brown coffin. I was always a little jealous he thought. I have to admit it. He always had been, a little, because although Ian made the slingshots, and invented the use of marbles instead of rocks, which tended to veer off target, it was Peter who dared to make a present of the squirrel's tail to the girls they lusted after and to tell them: "You wear them where we'll have to look for them." It was Ian who'd say, "The So'West must be pretty good by now," but it was Peter who knifed into it from a tree without even testing the water with his toe, scattering the surprised trout, taking a long slow swim underwater, and climbing out, red-skinned from head to toe. "Warm as toast," he'd say. You had to admire that. He had envied him. But not much or for long because he thought of him as a brother. More than a brother because sometimes you could hate your brother. "Holy Mary, mother of God, pray for us sinners, now and at the hour of our death, amen. Glory be to the Father and to the Son and to the Holy Ghost."

"Amen."

"De profundis clamo ad te, Domine."

"Domine audi vocem meam."   Everyone got up off their knees and sat in the chairs around the wall and prayed in silence, or chatted. Some went out to the kitchen for a cup of tea and to talk. At a wake, there are always people you never see any other time. Ian left the kneeling-bench in front of the coffin and walked over to Gloria's chair and sat on the arm. She was seated at the front edge of it as she was when he came in, her face in her hands. He put his finger on her shoulder.

"Hello Gloria," he said. She took her face out of her hands and put her thumbs under her chin and turned her head.

"Ian. I'm glad you came."

"How are you doing?"

"Terrible. Just terrible. My mother has to do every-thing! I should be doing things but every time I start even to talk I start to cry."

"You seem better now."

"Yes. This is the first time. The first dry words since they brought him home in that box. I didn't cry till then. I didn't believe it till then. But look, my eyes are dry now." They were dry, and brown, and large and round. Her ordeal had not harmed her beauty. If anything, she was better looking than he remembered. She was still small, but seemed more substantial, and dressed in black, she seemed older. Ian remembered her ambition to become a nun. All she needs now, he thought, is a cowl and a longer dress and she'd be one of the nuns who came to pray at her husband's wake.

"You look awful tired," he said.

"I am tired. I haven't slept since they brought him home."

"Why don't you go up and lie down for a while now?"

"Will you take me up?"

"Sure," he said, and they stood up, as if he had asked her to dance, and they faced each other for a moment. Sister Immaculata came over and put her gentle hands on their arms.

"I'm terribly sorry Gloria, you've had such trouble."

"Thank you Sister. It's awful, but I'll get over it; at least they tell me that."

"That's right, you know. You'll never forget it but you'll feel better as time goes by."

"She's going to go up and lie down for a while," Ian said.

"Oh that's good, Gloria, have a good rest. You'll need it."

Upstairs, lying on her back, her long brown hair splayed on the white pillow, she started to cry again as Ian looked down at her and tried to smile reassurance.

"Would you sit down beside me for a minute, Ian?" He sat.

"Would you hold my hand?" He took her hand and

held it on his thigh. Her eyes watered. "Can I tell you something?" she said.

"Yes."

"The last thing I said to him, I said: 'If you never come back, I don't give a shit!'"

"How come?"

"We were having an argument. About nothing of course."

"Well, you didn't mean it."

"No. But my God I said it."

"He'd know you didn't mean it."

"I feel guilty."

"You know you didn't mean it."

"I loved him."

"He'd have known that. He'd know you didn't mean it."

"Can I tell you something else, Ian?"

"Yes."

"I loved you a little too. Did you know that?"

"Yes."

"I couldn't tell you."

"I know."

"I feel guilty about that too."

"It doesn't matter if you feel it. You didn't do anything wrong. The feeling will go away."

"I hope so," she said. "I loved the both of you." She lifted her black dress and black slip and lifted Ian's hand and pushed it between her pale almost white thighs, above the tops of her black stockings. She said, "Don't worry, Ian, I wouldn't hurt you, be still." She closed her eyes and almost at once began to breathe deeply, her bosom rising and falling rhythmically, and her hands clasped together calmly on her belly. He became aware of silence, and then he could hear that the prayers had started again downstairs. "...blessed is the fruit of thy womb..." He wondered how anyone could wear garters tight around the legs; he couldn't stand even the elastics of stockings. "...pray for us sinners, now, and at the hour of our death..." He waited until he heard the final ejaculation: "Requiem aeternam dona ei, Domine: Ex lux perpetua luceat ei"; then he pulled his hand free, pulled Gloria's slip and dress over her knees, covered her with a quilt from the foot of the bed, walked downstairs, smiled and nodded at Sister Immaculata when she asked in a whisper if she was asleep. He went home.

Coming of Age in Canada

Marion Johnson

A. Evelyn's Tantrum

About Evelyn
This is a short, childish story about a six-year-old girl named Evelyn who lives in a very nice, medium-sized Canadian city with a lot of beautiful parks and other attractive facilities. Evelyn likes her nice city and her nice renovated house in the core area of the city and she likes all the nice friends that she has to play with at school. Evelyn thinks that her life is pretty good.

Even though Evelyn has no serious problems, her mother has quite a few. From time to time, Evelyn's mother disappears suddenly and then surfaces on a psychiatric ward, suffering from a mysterious emotional condition that no-one has been able to understand or explain, least of all the doctors. This has been going on for as long as Evelyn can remember, so she is fairly used to it now. Whenever her mother first goes into the hospital, there is a lot of trauma in the household and Evelyn herself has some difficulty sleeping. However, the hospital stays are getting shorter and in the weeks following any episode, Evelyn and her mother usually have quite a lot of fun together. The mother and daughter make excursions to the various parks around their city, enjoying a picnic or a skating outing, depending on the season when Evelyn's mother has gotten herself into difficulty. They regularly go into small restaurants where Evelyn has a strawberry milkshake while her mother drinks coffee and smokes cigarettes. Evelyn enjoys all of these outings as much as her mother does and she is secretly glad that her mother isn't capable of holding a regular job like some of the other kids' mothers at school. It makes her more available.

Evelyn's father is a mathematics teacher in a high school. His hobby is reading European and North American social history. Recognizing that his daughter is precocious, the father strives to encourage similar interests in her. For example, he has already told Evelyn all about the fact that in the bad old days, women were not allowed to attend universities or to study to become doctors and lawyers. The father has impressed upon Evelyn that these opportunities are now open to her and that she can realize whatever ambition she has in life, as long as she is prepared to work hard.

One of Evelyn's father's own ambitions is to purchase a

condominium in Florida, and he has various schemes about how he might afford it. Evelyn's mother says she doesn't want to live in Florida, she thinks winter isn't all that bad.

Evelyn and Billy
Everyone is agreed that Billy is a brat. Billy won't finish his class assignments, won't co-operate in athletic games and sings off-key at the top of his lungs. All the other children are fed up with him.

Evelyn is the opposite. She is a popular girl with children and teachers alike. She never talks back, never complains and always finishes her work neatly and on time. Miss Bradley, the teacher, is grateful to have Evelyn in her class. On the November report card, Miss Bradley wrote, "Evelyn is a charming girl and a real asset to the class." Again, in January, Miss Bradley wrote, "Evelyn is a tidy and well-mannered child with a natural aptitude for academic work. She gets along well with other children and is at the top of her class." These remarks made Evelyn's father so proud: he had such high hopes for his Evelyn.

The time is now early spring and thus far, Evelyn and Billy have had little to do with each other. Nevertheless, Billy seems to be interested in Evelyn. He often watches her on the playground and one time he offered her a stick of bubblegum. But as soon as she reached out to take it, Billy grabbed the gum away, chortling to himself. Anxious to hide her disappointment, Evelyn turned her back on him and walked away. She didn't pay any further attention to him for some time.

Evelyn's tantrum
It all happened quickly and was a great surprise to everybody. Evelyn decided that she would try to make up with

Billy because she didn't like to be on the outs with any-body. Evelyn sidled up to Billy on the playground and said to him in her sweetest manner, "Billy, would you like a piece of gum? My dad bought it for me and it's sugarless." Billy folded his arms over his chest and look-ing at her smugly said, "Yuck! I can't stand sugarless gum."

Right then Evelyn let him have it. She pounded away with both her fists and he must have had a few good bruises when it was over. Miss Bradley was on yard duty at the time. She spotted the commotion right away and soon put at end to it. "Evelyn," she said with some sever-ity, "nice girls don't hit."

"I hate Billy," said Evelyn. "He's a creep."

"If you don't like him," said Miss Bradley with final-ity, "then you just keep away from him. And Billy, you keep away from Evelyn." Miss Bradley had a way of mak-ing everything sound so simple.

After that, Evelyn rejoined the girls playing hop-scotch close to the school building while Billy retreated to a far corner of the playground. Even from that distance, Evelyn could tell that Billy was still smiling, tickled pink to have gotten her goat.

Sequel

Evelyn's parents talked the incident over with Miss Brad-ley at the final Parent / Teachers' Night at the school. It was Evelyn's father who brought the subject up—he didn't want Miss Bradley to get any wrong ideas about his Evelyn!

"Well, now," said Miss Bradley with an understanding smile, "I guess our Evelyn does have quite a little temper after all." This remark prompted Evelyn's mother to volunteer that there had been some pressures at home recently and perhaps this was what Evelyn was really reacting to. Miss Bradley looked puzzled but continued to smile politely. The mother then tried to reassure the teacher that everything was getting better, but in the end she just laughed about it and said, "Oh well, I've had a few good tantrums myself. I guess she's learning it from me." Evelyn's mother was really very understanding about kids.

Disclaimer
The author was never a violent child.

Questions for discussion
(1) Is Evelyn's mother getting enough help from the doctors?
(2) Will Evelyn grown up to be like her mother? Why or why not?

Comments
Commentator A—Billy is indeed a brat. What is interesting is his flair for drawing out the same quality in Evelyn.

The author appears to have a grudge against the psychiatric establishment although her story provides insufficient explanation for this. The questions cannot be answered on the basis of the facts presented in the story. Is this the author's first attempt at literature?
Commentator B—The story is not so simple or childish as it appears on the surface. There is evidence of humour. Billy is a natural anarchist but shows signs of becoming a serious student of human nature. He sees that Evelyn is a stuck-up prig who expects other people to conform to her narrow standards of behaviour while helping her to enhance her good opinion of herself. Billy deliberately undermines Evelyn's overblown self-image and in this he is doing her a favour—albeit a trifle unkindly.

Evelyn's mother is a masochist suffering from severe emotional repression. Her husband is either repressed himself or merely limited, and this would account for his apparent insensitivity to the mother's feelings. Evelyn acts strongly and directly on her feelings toward Billy and this provides some hope that she will grow up to be less emotionally disturbed than her mother.

I agree that the author appears to have a grudge against doctors. Is the story autobiographical?

Commentator C—The story evokes childhood romance with a charming simplicity. Let's give the author the benefit of the doubt and move on to the next story.

B. Mrs. Rollins' First Time in the Arctic

Background to the story

Howard Rollins met Elizabeth at a small get-acquainted party for faculty and incoming graduate students in the anthropology department. Howard was a 36-year-old bachelor at the time who worked hard and was already considered to be a distinguished member of the department. Howard had always been careful to avoid social entanglements with students and he had never dated any woman in his department, faculty or student. But the chemistry with Elizabeth was instant and overpowering and Howard knew before the evening was over that he wanted to marry her.

The attraction would hardly have surprised many people. Elizabeth was a beautiful girl and dressed smartly for a graduate student, because she had been working for a few years and had developed a good wardrobe for herself. Elizabeth was 26. She also felt an immediate attraction to Howard.

Under the circumstances, it was too embarrassing to offer Elizabeth a lift home, so instead Howard just invited her to drop by his office the next day to talk over her choice of course-work. She did so, and this was the real beginning of their relationship. After they had chatted for a while, Elizabeth made a few polite inquiries about the graduate course Howard was offering that fall. Anticipating a tricky dilemma for himself, Howard decided to go out on a limb. "Look here, Elizabeth," he said with some feeling, "I'd far rather take you to dinner than enroll you in my graduate course. So perhaps you would be best advised to stick with Helen Smith's course on Structuralism." Howard had a way of going for the jugular on occasion; some colleagues believed that this was the key to his success in anthropology.

"To be honest," replied Elizabeth, "I don't much care which course I take. But dinner will have to be on Saturday night because I'm already booked for Friday." Elizabeth had never been all that shy around men; why should she be when Howard made his feelings so plain?

After that, Howard and Elizabeth were a steady affair, and Howard had to put up with occasional sly looks and subtle digs from his peers. In the spring the couple were quietly married and Elizabeth set about energetically transforming Howard's bachelor house into a cosy family home. Elizabeth decided to complete her MA program but she told everybody that she wasn't sure what she would do after that, especially when she discovered in November that she was pregnant. Nothing Howard had said could slow Elizabeth down over the pregnancy: she pointed out to him most emphatically that anthropology could wait, but in a few years they would both be getting too old for babies. Howard felt she had a point there. It was hard enough adjusting to his prospective new status in life at the age of 37.

This is just about all there is to tell about the beginning of the marriage. Howard and Elizabeth were together for the birth of Brian and it was the most thrilling moment of their lives. Elizabeth stayed home after that and she was deliriously happy for the first few months. However, when Brian was around six months old, he changed from a relatively placid to a fussy baby, especially at night, and Elizabeth was beginning to feel tired much of the time. Also, she felt rather housebound because the winter weather kept the two indoors so much. Consequently, when Howard started talking about making a six-week trip to the Arctic as soon as the term was over, Elizabeth was adamant that she wanted to go too. She needed a break, she told Howard, some new adventure in her life; and besides, she couldn't bear the thought of their being separated for such a long time.

This was a new situation for Howard. He was accustomed to operating on his own in any field situation and he had an established modus vivendi that had always worked well for him. Nevertheless, the idea appealed to him. Taking along his new family would help to humanize his image in the community he worked in, and at any rate, it would certainly cut down on the loneliness he inevitably felt as an outsider in an isolated area. So Howard agreed to take Elizabeth and Brian with him, but he tactfully suggested that she leave behind her high heels and other fancy duds. "You won't be needing *them*," he said laughing. "After all, we don't want the native boys going too wild over you." Howard was so proud of Elizabeth, and of baby Brian too, of course.

The story
"Is this your first time in the North, Mrs. Rollins?" A burly, smiling man in a heavy parka, open at the throat, stepped forward from the cluster of men at the foot of the plane steps and grasped Elizabeth warmly by the hand. Elizabeth shifted Brian more firmly onto her left hip and

tried to return the warmth of his grasp. She couldn't help feeling a bit nervous about her first trip to the Arctic.

Before Elizabeth could gather her wits to reply to the man, her husband stepped up behind her and the man's attention quickly shifted to him. "Welcome, Professor Rollins," he boomed. "We hope this is going to be a good research trip for you." Howard Rollins smiled amiably and said, "Hello, Jensen, hello. It's good to meet you at last. I'm so glad to be here because I always enjoy visiting the Arctic."

Howard Rollins had come to this tiny Arctic settlement to do a small research project on Inuit material culture and hopefully, to provide the Inuit there with a little technical assistance on how to record their own culture and traditions. The local arrangements for the expedition had been made through Mr. Jensen, who had been in the North for some years and who took an amateur interest in anthropology himself.

The airport building was small and it wasn't long before they were through with the preliminaries. Elizabeth could hear snatches of Inuktitut from the clusters of Inuit people around her, and the sound of the language was strangely intriguing to her. It was the sound of the language that made her feel she was truly in the Canadian North.

Once they had retrieved all of their personal belongings and Howard's voluminous research files, Mr. Jensen quickly bundled them all into the cab of his pickup truck. It was cosy and really warm inside because of all the crowding. Elizabeth felt happy and she cuddled Brian close to her. He seemed to be enjoying himself too.

Mr. Jensen was a social worker and he had a pretty tough job in a community like that. But he was a realist and had already survived three years in the same place, so the people there liked him and they asked him to stay on.

He said he was glad to do so, although he was concerned about the education of his children in the North. But for the time being, the Jensens were determined to stay on.

The plan was for the Rollinses to stay with the Jensens for a few weeks while Howard worked out of an office the school was willing to provide. It had all been arranged through a friend of a friend and Elizabeth hoped they wouldn't be crowding the Jensens right out of their home. She didn't like crowded conditions much herself but of course she would have to put up with it. In the end, this positive attitude proved to be the right response and everything worked out really well at the Jensen's house.

The Jensens had a dinner party for the Rollinses soon after their arrival, inviting a few of their closest friends. The group included Beverly Arnitok and her Inuit husband Johnny; the school principal and his rather mousey-looking wife; and Valery, an unattached nurse on a two-year contract who was a close friend of Mrs. Jensen's. Valery was a plain and quiet girl but nevertheless Elizabeth liked her right away and felt at ease in her company.

The Arnitoks were an especially interesting couple. He had an important position with the town council and she stayed home with the kids. Beverly was completely crazy over Johnny and it was easy to tell that Johnny was crazy over her too. The couple already had four children and they both spent a lot of time with the kids and were really devoted to them and to each other. Naturally, there must have been strains due to the cultural differences within the home, but to Elizabeth they seemed like an ideal family.

While everyone was still enjoying dinner together, Mr. Jensen (having imbued himself with a more than healthy amount of wine) suddenly leaped up and proposed a toast to his good new friends, the Rollinses. He said how they needed a little fresh blood in such a small community from time to time and how everyone was very pleased to welcome them here. Jensen finished off by giving Elizabeth a friendly hug and winking across the table at his wife.

Just one small incident marred the party a little bit for Elizabeth. Late in the evening, the school principal made a mild pass at her in the back bedroom. He said he just wanted to fondle her breasts (maybe he was impotent), and he was very sweet about it. She let him down as gently as possible and went to check on baby Brian as soon as she could get away.

Once Howard's research project got into full swing, he didn't have much time for anything else and Elizabeth was left to her own resources. With Mrs. Jensen efficiently keeping house for everybody, there wasn't much for Elizabeth to do—other than care for Brian, of course. However, she found that she liked just hanging around the settlement and trying to learn as much as possible about life there. She was finding that it was easy to meet people and get into conversation with them and the whole experience was turning into quite a holiday for her. She was glad she had come along and it wasn't boring at all for her.

Through Mrs. Jensen, Elizabeth started getting friendly with the nurse Valery, and she regularly went over to Valery's apartment whenever Valery was off work. Elizabeth always took Brian with her and Valery really enjoyed playing with him. Naturally, the conversation almost always came around to men and sex! They sometimes found themselves giggling like a pair of schoolgirls as they gossiped about who might be attracted to whom in the settlement. They got so friendly that Elizabeth even confided to Valery that dreadful incident with the school principal. Then they couldn't help laughing at the poor guy, although they both felt sorry for his wife.

Elizabeth had been reading a bit of anthropology and she sometimes brought that into the conversation, too. For example, one time she raised the topic of shamanism. "Valery," she said, suddenly girlish and enthused, "wouldn't it have been exciting in the old days to sleep with a shaman?! I bet they really knew how to do it. I bet they could seduce a woman utterly just with their eyes."

"Yes," said Valery. "I read somewhere once that in the old days a shaman could have any woman he wanted. I bet some of them had plenty of women."

"I agree," said Elizabeth. "I wonder how the husbands felt about that?" As she said this, she suddenly noticed that Brian was trying to pull himself upright on the small coffee-table holding the teapot and she rushed to pull him away. Valery shared her alarm and moved the teapot and the two mugs to a safer location.

One day Howard, wanting to be helpful, said to Elizabeth, "Darling, if you have your own interests in Inuit culture, why don't you talk to Beverly Arnitok's husband? He's a knowledgeable fellow and he seems quite supportive of anthropological work."

So the next evening they arranged to visit the Arnitoks and when she had the opportunity, Elizabeth cornered Johnny on a question about family life in traditional times. Johnny seemed quite responsive and they chatted for quite a while about the problem. Gradually Howard and Beverly were drawn into the discussion as well and they all had quite a time. When the Rollinses left, Johnny assured Elizabeth that he would be happy to talk to her again some time, and Beverly agreed that it was a good idea for them all to get together, she had found it all so very interesting herself.

In one of their subsequent conversations, Elizabeth told Johnny that what she was really most curious about was shamanism. "I've always been interested in magic," she said, "ever since I was a little girl." Johnny looked surprised and he said, "Have you told your husband about this?"

"No, I haven't," she replied defensively, surprised in turn at his question. "He's not very interested in religious ideas. I'm the one who wants to talk about it." Johnny looked dubious. "I think you'd better leave that one alone, Elizabeth," he said. "That's all in the past now and people are afraid to talk about it. You better just forget that topic." Elizabeth didn't like Johnny telling her what to do so authoritatively but she understood that he knew more about the subject than she did, so she wisely decided to drop it altogether.

One day Elizabeth went over to Valery's apartment by herself. Baby Brian was happily playing with the Jensen children, under the capable supervision of Mrs. Jensen, and Elizabeth had felt that she would just like to get away from the noise of children for a while. Mrs. Jensen kindly urged her to take advantage of the opportunity, so Elizabeth wandered over to Valery's by herself. She was surprised to find Johnny Arnitok there. Johnny worked in an office close by and he explained that he sometimes dropped in on Valery for his tea-break; Valery baked such good cookies, he said laughing.

They all chatted pleasantly together for a while and then the telephone rang. It was the nursing-station calling to say that an Inuit boy had been brought in badly hurt and could Valery please help out. Of course, Valery was determined to go down there immediately, but she urged the others to finish their tea.

When the door had closed on Valery, the room suddenly became very quiet. Elizabeth looked at Johnny and Johnny looked back at her. The eye contact lasted only a moment because Johnny raised his eyebrows, and that prompted Elizabeth to query, "Does Beverly make good cookies, too?"

The question made Johnny laugh more openly than Elizabeth had ever heard him do before, and she laughed too out of sheer relief that she hadn't made a complete fool of herself. Finally Johnny said, "Actually, I prefer bannock with raisins and she's quite good at that." They were both quick-witted in that tricky situation.

After that, Johnny left quickly to get back to his office and Elizabeth wandered up to the school to see Howard. Howard was having a tea-break with his Inuit co-workers and he was very happy to see Elizabeth.

Two weeks later the Rollins family left town, not knowing if they would ever see their Arctic friends again. In the taxi en route to the airport, Howard told Elizabeth that it had been one of his best field trips ever and he hoped that in future he could always take her and Brian with him to the field. He said he had learned that a man really needed his family close by under such stressful conditions. Then he added jokingly, "You have to become very mature to survive in such a climate." Howard could be very funny sometimes. He was a good man and really tried hard to be helpful to other people.

Epilogue
The Eskimo taxi driver who took Howard and Elizabeth to the airport seemed to appreciate Howard's little joke, and he smiled to himself. He actually spoke better English than the Rollinses had realized.

Disclaimer
The author has never had any deep conversations with Inuit men.

(1) What is the most surprising turn of events in the story?

(2) Is Howard helpful?

(3) Should Elizabeth have offered to help Mrs. Jensen with the housework?

Comments

Commentator A—It would be interesting to know if the shamans were all that attractive to women. Elizabeth's remarks on this betray an immature personality with an adolescent sexual curiosity. Johnny likewise appears to be naive. Hence it is a surprising turn of events when they don't take advantage of the opportunity to act out their feelings of attraction to each other.

I don't think Howard was all that helpful to Elizabeth when they were in the Arctic, but in the end this did not matter too much. Perhaps he was more successful in helping his Inuit co-workers.

There is no evidence that Mrs. Jensen wanted help with the housework.

Commentator B—The author provides a sympathetic portrayal of Johnny Arnitok as an intelligent, responsible and attractive young man. It is hardly surprising that he betrays some vulnerability to Elizabeth's seductiveness but, taking the whole situation into account, I was not especially surprised that he ultimately recognized the flirtation for what it was. Elizabeth's case is somewhat more complex: she starts out with a frivolous interest in sensitive topics but recognizes quite rapidly the moral value of bringing her curiosity under control. This is a lot for an attractive young woman to learn on her first trip to the Arctic and so the story loses credibility.

Howard is less helpful than he wants to be but he shows some capacity for learning from his mistakes. I think that Mrs. Jensen definitely needed help with all that housework.

Commentator C—I agree with Panel Member B. To sum up, the marital score-card can be given as follows:

the Rollinses—A + (naturally); this couple is developing a good understanding of their responsibilities and the limitations these impose

the Arnitoks—B + ; a good effort, with some room for improvement

the Jensens—a steady C + ; all that crowding seems to have kept Jensen in line

the principal and his wife—D − ; a near miss

Valery may be unattached for a long time.

C. Alice and Abraham

This is a short, simple story of a sociologist named Alice who as a graduate student had gotten married to a talented physicist, also a serious student of life. Unfortunately, the marriage didn't work out and anxious to forget her disappointment, Alice decided to devote her life to the study of human societies. She was not considered by her colleagues to be a great sociologist but she was quite good and she was generally well-received in the academic world and in all the communities where she worked.

One year she decided to do a small research project on Cape Breton Island. She had always wanted to experience that part of the country so she arranged to spend a summer studying some of the folkways of the Cape Breton Islanders. The whole experience turned out to be quite a bit more than she had originally bargained for, but still, it was worth it.

At first nothing much seemed to happen to Alice on the Island, although the folkways project was going quite well. Then she chanced to meet Abraham, a New York Jew who had renounced his former affluent lifestyle and come to live on Cape Breton Island as a simple fisherman. He was a great storyteller and loved poking fun at academics, imitating some of their worst pomposities with surprising accuracy. Occasionally, Abraham went a little too far and really hurt Alice's feelings, because he seemed to be suggesting that Alice herself was a bit foolish. But Alice chose to overlook his shenanigans because he always made the game seem playful rather than vicious; and besides, she had a secret suspicion that he might be right about how pompous she herself could be. It helped to put things into perspective for her, so she forgave him every time.

Naturally, Alice went to bed with Abraham the first time he jumped on her. There was no reason to hold back, and it was too good to miss, for both of them. It was still a bit of a surprise to Alice when it happened, however, because she had never once imagined that she was especially attracted to Americans or to Jews.

Once Alice started sleeping with Abraham, she started losing some of her motivation to work so hard and the folkways project started to go downhill. But she decided not to worry about it; she was almost 40 and she felt she had worked hard enough in her life—her career was secure enough for the time being. She needed a holiday and Abraham was certainly giving her that!

The story of what happened between Alice and Abraham is not that complex or original: at the end of the summer, Abraham asked Alice to marry him and live as a fisherman's wife on the Island. She could continue a little sociology on the side if she really wanted to and he swore he would always be supportive of that. She said she would have to think it over and went back to Toronto.

Classes resumed in September and continued until the

end of April, so Alice was pretty busy with that. But Abraham was still on Alice's mind and at Christmas she went back to Cape Breton for another week's holiday. She knew there was no chance that Abraham would come to Toronto for Christmas! He no longer had any interest in big cities or Christmas, but he did insist on sending her the money for the fare. He said he felt it was only right, even if she did make more money than he did nowadays.

By the end of April, Alice knew that she was facing the most momentous decision of her life. She decided to write a letter to Abraham, and the first time she tried, this is what she wrote:

Dear Abraham,
I am writing to tell you that I am still thinking over your offer and I hope it still stands. I hate to admit this, but the problem is that I have so much invested in my career. It's hard to imagine that I could give it all up completely and always be happy as a fisherman's wife. I'm just not sure so I still can't say yes to you even though I think you are the most wonderful man I ever met.
Yours affectionately,
Alice

Alice put the letter away for a while because she didn't feel quite right about it. After a time, she decided that she would try to approach the subject matter differently —in the teasing and playful manner he loved so much. That ought to get the message across.

Dear Abraham, (she wrote)
I love you so much that I have decided to accept your proposal and quit my job at the university right away. In order to keep myself occupied until we can have the

baby (I hope it's not too late!), I plan to write a book about the sex lives of the Cape Breton Island fishermen. I plan to collect as much concrete data as possible and publish it in a book for the general public. Would you like to co-operate in this project and can you suggest any other fishermen who might be interested? I will of course pay them a decent wage for their services.

As always, waiting anxiously for your reply—

Alice

The third and last time she tried to write to Abraham, Alice wrote as follows:

Dear Abraham,

There is an opening for a sociologist at a minor college on the Nova Scotia mainland. Do you want me to apply for it?

Yours hopefully,

Alice

In the end, Alice couldn't decide what to do about the three letters she had written. So she set them aside in a secret file and waited to see what would develop the next time she heard from Abraham.

Resolution to the story

Just before the end of term, the chairman of Alice's department was injured in a car accident and Alice was asked to fill in as the acting chairman. Alice did well at the job and she soon discovered that she loved the challenge and prestige of her new position; it really was too much to give up. Reluctantly, Alice broke off with Abraham and rededicated her life to the social sciences. Two years later, Alice was appointed to a regular term as chairman of her department. Coincidentally, at about the same time she met up with a very nice economist from a small town in Arizona. Romance came back into Alice's life and the couple were soon living in comfortable common-law. As far as the author can tell, this couple will remain together as long as the economist does not decide to retire to his home-town.

Meanwhile, Abraham has married a beautiful Micmac woman who has never been off Cape Breton Island except to consult medical specialists in Halifax. This woman already had three children and she has had three more by Abraham, so he is kept pretty busy trying to support his family on a fisherman's income. It is a happy life for Abraham and he always remembers Alice with a great deal of affection.

No questions, this story is quite straightforward. No disclaimer necessary.

Comments

Commentator A—The character of Abraham is reminiscent of Billy, and Alice is the woman that Evelyn could become. Alice's original attraction to Abraham may have been motivated by a fear of success. The resolution is appropriate because an ambitious professional woman like Alice could never fit happily into an existence on the fringes of the modern world.

Commentator B—Alice enjoys feeling important more than she enjoys being laughed at. Recognizing this fact, she made a sensible choice for her life.

Commentator C—Alice's letters to Abraham express considerable one-upmanship. Since it is clear that Abraham never intends to let her get the upper hand, she was wise to back off from the relationship.

Autobiographical note
The author of these stories is a former teacher of English composition and linguistics who took very early retirement. She lives in London, Ontario and has travelled to a number of interesting places within Canada, including Rankin Inlet in the Northwest Territories and Port Morien on Cape Breton Island. She has a daughter who is five years old and is, like her mother, fairly mature for her age although they both regularly throw temper tantrums, occasionally in public.

Django, Karfunkelstein & Roses

Norman Levine

In late October, on the morning of my fiftieth birthday, we had breakfast early—my wife and three daughters. On the plain wooden table: a black comb, a half-bottle of brandy, a red box of matches from Belgium, a felt-tip pen, a couple of Dutch cigars, a card of Pissarro's *Lower Norwood Under Snow* and a record. They wished me happy birthday. And we kissed.

After breakfast the children went to school. We continued to talk, without having to finish sentences, over another cup of coffee. Then my wife went to make the beds, water the plants, do the washing. And I went to the front-room, lit the coal fire, smoked a Dutch cigar, drank some of the brandy, put the record on, listened to Django Reinhardt and Stephane Grappelli—The Hot Club of France. And looked out for the postman.

The mimosa tree was still in bloom in the small front garden as were some roses. To the left, a road of terraced houses curved as it sloped down to the church steeple and the small shops. And at the end of the road—above houses, steeple, shops—was the white-blue water of the bay.

Directly opposite, past the garden and across the road, was Wesley Street. A short narrow street of stone cottages. I watched the milkman leave bottles on the granite by the front doors. Mr. Veal—a tall man with glasses, a retired carpenter, a Plymouth brethren ("I have my place up there when I die," he told me pointing to the sky)—came out of his cottage holding a white tablecloth. He shook the tablecloth in the street. From the slate roofs, the red chimney pots, came jackdaws, sparrows and a few gulls. They were waiting for him. Mr. Veal swirled the tablecloth—as if it were a cape—and over his shoulder it folded neatly on his back. He stood in the centre of the street with the white tablecloth on his back, the birds near his feet ("I need to get wax out of my ears," he said when we were walking. "I don't hear people—but I hear the birds"). Then he went inside.

The postman appeared and walked past the house. This morning it didn't matter. My wife hung the washing in the courtyard and pulled up the line. Then left the house to buy the food for our day. The sun came through the coloured glass of the inside front door and onto the floor in shafts of soft yellow, blue and red. I went upstairs to the large attic room. And got on with the new story...

Within a few years this life changed. And for my wife it ended. The children left home. I would get up early—the gulls woke me—wondering what to do (I wasn't writing anything). Living by oneself like this, I thought, how long the day is. How slow it goes by. I went from one empty room to another...looked outside...such a nice-looking place...and wondered how to go on. And there were times when I wondered why go on?

Then a letter came from Zurich. It came from the people who worked in a literary agency. They told me that my literary agent was going to be 70. They were planning a surprise party. Could I come?

At the airport a young man with curly brown hair and glasses, just over medium height, was holding a sheet of paper with my name on it. He was shy (no, he hadn't been waiting long). He smiled easily. He said he did the accounts.

"You have not met Ruth?"

"No," I said.

"How long is she your agent?"

"Fourteen years."

Zurich was busy. In sunny end-of-May weather he drove to the heights above...to a *cul-de-sac* of large houses. They had signs, *Achtung Hund*...except in front of the large house where he stopped.

As he opened the door there were red roses, in the hallway, lots of them. And more red roses at the bottom of the wide stairs. The wall opposite the front door was mostly books. But in a space, waist high, a small sink with the head of a brass lion. Water came out of its mouth. There were more roses, as well as books, in the large carpeted rooms that he led me through. Then outside, down a few steps, to a grass lawn. People were standing in clusters talking and eating. A tall attractive woman with straight blond hair was cooking over a bar-

becue. She talked loudly in Italian. A man in his thirties
—regular clean-cut face, black curly hair—was moving
around slowly with a handheld camera, stopping, then
moving again.

The person at the airport came toward me with a lively
short woman. She looked very alert, intelligent and with
a sense of fun.

"What a surprise," she said. We embraced quickly and
kissed. Then we moved apart and looked at one another.

"This is very moving," she said quietly.

I could hear the whirr of the film camera.

"You must be hungry."

She linked arms, led me to the barbecue and introduced me to Giuli—the tall blond Italian who was her
housekeeper. (She would die, unexpectedly, in two
years.) There were frankfurters, hamburgers, salad,
grapes. I had a couple of frankfurters and walked to the
lawn's edge and to an immediate drop. The churches, the
buildings, the houses of Zurich spread out below and in
front. Across some water I could see wooded hills. And
further away, hardly visible against the skyline, mountains.

More people kept arriving. I could now hear French
and German. It was pleasantly warm. Sparrows flitted
around us. Giuli, and others, threw them bits of bread.

That night cars brought the guests into Zurich. The
birthday party was in a Guildhall near the centre. A narrow river was outside. The water looked black, I could see
several white swans on it. The guests came from different
parts of Western Europe. They were mostly publishers.
But I did meet Alfred Andersch. A gentle man with a
pleasant face, a nice smile. ("Why write novels if you can
write short stories?") He would die within a year. And
Elias Canetti. A short stocky man with a large face, high

forehead, thick black hair brushed back. (He would be awarded the Nobel Prize.)

There were speeches, toasts, in English. Then the guests went in line to another room where—on a long table with white tablecloths—there were lit candles and all sorts of food. Platters of shrimp...asparagus...a large cooked salmon...roast beef...the salads were colourful. I looked ahead to the far end where the cakes were. And saw, on the table, what I thought was one of the white swans from the river. As I came closer I realized it was made of butter.

Later that night, in the house, seven of us who were staying as guests sat with Ruth in the kitchen. We talked and drank. I was the only male. The women's ages spread from the late thirties into the seventies. The youngest was the girl from upstairs who rented a room and worked in Zurich. She was waiting for her gentleman friend to phone to let her know when he would be in Zurich. After she spoke to him she came down and joined us and she started to sing "It's All Right With Me." She had a fine voice. We joined in. There were more Cole Porter songs. And Jerome Kern. Then the older ladies sang, very enthusiastically, European socialist songs. And went on to folk songs, mostly German (Ruth was born in Hamburg). The one that made an impression was a slow sad tune about the black death.

Giuli, sitting beside me, said in broken English how her husband, a pilot in the Italian air force, was killed while flying. And how lucky she was to find Ruth. Then, with more wine, she began to talk Italian to everyone and stood up wanting us all to dance. We formed a chorus line, Ruth in the middle. We kicked our legs up and sang as we moved around the kitchen. Then, tired, we sat down. This time Ruth was beside me, a little out of breath. While our glasses were being filled again I asked her—what was she thinking when she saw those large bunches of roses all over the house?

And she said, that during the last war she worked as a courier for the resistance. They sent her to Holland. The Nazis tracked her down. "Things became difficult. I was on a wanted list. I had to stay inside my small room. I couldn't go out.

"In the next room there was a man called Karfunkelstein. He told me he was going to commit suicide. I asked him why.

"'One can't live with a name like Karfunkelstein in these times.'

"I managed to talk him out of it.

"'Wait,' he said. And left me.

"When he came back he had his arms full of roses and other flowers.

"'For you,' he said.

"And gave them to me.

"My small room was full of flowers. And I couldn't go out to sell a rose for food."

Four and a half years later, early this December, I saw Ruth again. I had been invited to Strasbourg to give a lecture at the university. After the lecture I took a train to Zurich. Outside the station I went into a waiting taxi. I gave the driver the name of the street.

He replied with the number I wanted.

"How did you know?"

"Many people go there."

This time no guests or flowers. But the same warm welcome. The young man who met me at the airport was still doing the accounts, still looked shy and smiled easily. His hair was grey. I met the new housekeeper, Juliette. She came from France. About the same age as Ruth.

It was cold and foggy. At dusk I could see the lights of Zurich below. Juliette brought in some coffee and for over an hour Ruth and I talked business. She phoned up the Canadian embassy in Bonn and spoke to the cultural attaché about an East German translation. She phoned a radio station in Cologne about a short story that had been broadcast. We went over a contract line by line. Then Ruth said.

"I must go and lie down for twenty minutes."

She went upstairs. I went into the kitchen. And talked to Juliette while she was preparing the food. Juliette told me she used to be a photographer in Paris before the war. Then worked in London. She had a studio in Knightsbridge. And talked nostalgically of the time she lived there. A small radio was on. Someone was playing a guitar. I said I liked Django Reinhardt.

"I knew him," Juliette said. "My husband Andre was his best friend for some years."

Ruth appeared looking less tired.

"You didn't stay twenty minutes," Juliette said in mock anger.

Ruth and I finished the rest of our business over a drink. Then it was time for supper. The three of us sat around a small table in the kitchen, in a corner, by the stove. We had red wine. We clinked glasses and drank to our next meeting.

Juliette passed the salad bowl.

I asked her about Django Reinhardt.

"He couldn't read or write. He was a gypsy," she said. "Very black hair but good white teeth. You know how he got those two fingers? His wife was in a caravan making artificial flowers when there was a fire. Django ran in and saved her. His hand was burned.... Oh, he was a bad driver. He had so many accidents...the car looked a wreck. One time he came to see us with a new shirt, a tie and a new suit. He asked my husband what was the proper way to wear it? Andre showed him. Django stood in front of the mirror wearing the new clothes, looking at himself, very pleased at the way he looked." (Juliette acted this out with little movements of her face and hands as she spoke.) "We listened to him play...he would play for hours...if I could have recorded it... He only began to make records so he could give them to his friends. But he could be difficult. To get him to the recording-studio on time my husband would say 'Django, you are late...the machinery is all set up...there are people waiting...they have their jobs.' And Django would not go. Andre tried again. And Django got angry.

"'I need my freedom. If I can't have my freedom...it's not my life.'

"Later he bought a Chateau near Paris. That life didn't suit him. He was ruined...by money...by women... fame. He couldn't handle it."

Juliette stood up and from the stove brought a small casserole and served the meat and vegetables.

"What happened to Karfunkelstein?" I asked Ruth.

"He probably committed suicide," she said in a flat voice. "In those days people like him did...

"On May tenth, 1940," she went on, "the Germans came into Holland. Next day there was an epidemic of suicides. There weren't enough coffins. They put them in sacks.

"I knew this young family. They had two small boys. The man was a teacher. His wife was in love with him. She would go along with whatever he wanted. And he wanted to commit suicide. He kept saying: 'Life as it is going to be...will not be worth living.'

"I knew someone in the American Embassy. I arranged for them to see him next morning so they could get out of Holland. But I wanted to make sure they would be there.

"I went to their house. The man was still saying that life without freedom to live the way he had lived would be impossible...when the younger boy swallowed a small bulb from a flashlight. (At least his mother said that he did.) She was very worried. She asked me: What should she do? How could she get a doctor? After a while the child got better. Because I saw how worried she had been I thought it was all right to leave them for the night. I said I would be back in the morning.

"When I arrived the two boys were dead. The man and the wife had sealed all the doors and windows. Turned on the gas. And they had cut their wrists."

When we had finished, Juliette began to clear and wash up while Ruth went into the other room to dictate letters into a machine for the secretary next morning. I went up to the room where I would sleep the night—a large bare room in the attic with a low double bed, books all over and a wide window with a view of Zurich. I looked at the lights and thought of the people who had come to Zurich, from other countries, for different reasons. And how few of them stayed.

Juliette came to the door and said, "There is a Canadian film on television. Have you heard of it? It is called *Mon Oncle Antoine*."

"It's the best Canadian film I have seen," I said.

"Then we shall all see it," she said.

I went down with her.

Juliette drew the curtains. Ruth put in a hearing-aid. "I only do this for television," she said.

I looked forward to seeing the film again. I had seen it, about twenty years ago, in St Ives on television and remembered how moved I had been by it.

"There is a marvellous shot," I said while the news was on. "It is winter. On the extreme left of the picture there is a horse and a sleigh with a young boy and his uncle. The horse has stopped. And on the extreme right of the picture is a coffin that has fallen off the sleigh. In between there is this empty field of snow. It is night. The wind is blowing...no words spoken. But that image I have remembered all these years."

Mon Oncle Antoine came on. The first surprise—it was in colour. I remembered it in black and white. Then I realized...it was because in St Ives we had then a black-and-white TV set. There were other disappointments. It might have been because of the German subtitles, or my memory.

I told them the scene was about to come on.

When it did—it wasn't memorable at all.

Was it because it was in colour? Or had it been cut? I remembered it as lasting much longer. And it was the length of the shot, in black-and-white, that made it so poignant.

When the film was over I could see they were disappointed.

"I remember it differently," I said. And told them how I had seen it on a black-and-white TV set.

"It would have been better in black-and-white," Ruth said.

"There may have been cuts."

"It seemed very jumpy," Juliette said. "You could see it had the possibility of a good movie."

That night in the attic, in bed, I heard midnight by the different clocks in Zurich. I didn't count how many. But there were several, each one starting a few seconds after another...and thought about *Mon Oncle Antoine.* How it differed from what I remembered. I saw how I had changed that shot. Just as I had switched the candles from around the man in the coffin at the start. And had them around the boy in the coffin at the end. I had, over the years, changed these things in order to remember them. Is this what time does? Perhaps it was a good film because it could suggest these things.

And was this what Juliette had done when she told about Django Reinhardt? And Ruth with Karfunkelstein?

But some things don't change.

I remember my wife having to go into Penzance hospital to drain off some fluid. It was in the last two weeks of her life. She hadn't been outside for over a year but in that front-room where I brought down a bed. And from there she looked at the granite of Wesley Street and Mr. Veal feeding the birds. Two men carried her out on a canvas and put her in the back of the ambulance.

When she returned she said, "It's so beautiful. The sky...the clouds...the trees...the fields...the hedges. I was lying on my back and I could see through the windows..."

Early next morning Ruth drove me to the railway station. The streets were quite empty. The sun was not high above the horizon. And here it was snowing. The sun caught the glass of the buildings, the houses, and lit them up. And the snow was falling...thick flakes.

"My aunt in Israel is 90," Ruth said. "And drives her car. Isn't that marvellous."

We were going down a turning road, down a slope, then it straightened out. I asked her:

"Will you go on living in Zurich?"

"I don't know. The only other country would be Holland. I like Holland."

After she left I went inside the station and gave all the Swiss change I had to a plump young girl who was selling things from a portable kiosk. In return I had a bar of chocolate, a large green apple and a pack of five small cigars.

119

Moths

Carol Windley

Joanna, behind the windows of her house, knows what it means to be alone. Nothing moves outside, anywhere, unless she counts the occasional swift wing of a heron or a hawk, glancing past in the fog. The fog rises from the lake, morning and evening, and drapes itself everywhere, a cold, tattered wet shawl.

Not that Joanna finds the fog cold and wet; she is entirely removed from what she sees, and can't even imagine what it would be like to touch the fog, or those dark high branches, or those clouds, or the cold lake water. She touches only glass; it keeps her in, holds her upright in her house. Joanna is only two eyes, taking in the unknowable, giving nothing back.

It isn't what she wanted.

And yet, what a commendable, what a fine individual Joanna is. Even though the hollow sound of her feet on the endless floors follows her, dogs her, haunts her, she is able to walk in the most ordinary paths: to the washer with dirty clothes, to the closets with clean clothes, to the chill ceramic distances of this vast new, extravagant new, kitchen. She walks and walks, stopping only for the most well earned breaks, then perching on the edge of a chair with her mug of coffee cradled in her hands. Staring out the windows. Fifteen minutes. Well then, 25 minutes. Timed, in careful imitation of what she is used to, what she was used to, not so very long ago.

She is lonely, but she functions well. His dinner is always ready, perfectly ready, well before the appointed time.

And then.

He is home, swooping up the drive, headlights drilling the dusk, machine-gunning the black cedars, ripping holes in the fog, pre-empting the dark.

Slam goes the car door. The garage door. The house door. The hall-closet door.

Joanna holds her breath. She wants to run and hide, wants to hold her breath, choke back excited, nervous laughter. Nobody home, nobody home. Find me, catch me if you can.

He says Hello, drops his suit jacket across a chair back, smiles, is happily redolent of the city, of town and travel; the warmth, the smell, the casual wonder of human sociability is all about him.

Joanna has not spoken aloud since seven o'clock in the morning, when she said goodbye to him. Eleven hours.

She tries her tongue against the roof of her mouth. Hello, she says. It sounds all right; it is not the chirp of a bird, the grunt of an animal. If it isn't quite the warm welcome of a loving wife either, what does it matter. The small frown that appears on his smooth handsome face is quickly gone, quickly gone. He rubs his hands together, as if in satisfaction. He carefully rolls his sleeves up to the elbow, shedding the skin of the city for the skin of the country, and home. Changing skins, changing colours, changing habitat. No trick at all.

Joanna knows that now she is supposed to ask him if he had a good day, but she doesn't. She is learning to be cruel in small ways; to get even. She watches Elliot wander around with his wine glass in his hand, smiling and nodding at the walls, the terra cotta, the polished oak.

There are five lighted candles in the candelabrum (Elliot prefers to dine by candelight) and five answering flames in the black sheet of glass behind the dining-room table. Joanna has not yet managed to order drapery material for all the windows, although she promises Elliot that she is working on it: it is just a matter of finding the right fabric, in the right shade. It is a matter of being absolutely sure, she tells Elliot. The truth is, she is never ready to drive into town with Elliot in the morning. She sleeps restlessly all night, then falls into a heavy sleep just before dawn. Hard to believe that a short time ago she was up at six o'clock five mornings a week. Oh, she is filled with nostalgia, with love, for that remembered exuberance, that purposefulness. She was another person then, that was a different lifetime. But it wasn't. It was only five months ago.

"Dear God," Joanna says. Her fork clatters onto her plate. Elliot's head snaps up, he follows the direction of her horrified gaze to the window, where the five flames are reflected. "What? What?" he demands, scraping his chair across the floor. He crouches, alarmed.

Joanna points. "Oh God, Elliot. Look."

He looks. "Moths?" he says, and straightens up, hands on his hips.

Moths. What Joanna sees are four or five creatures. Well, they are moths, but huge and bug-eyed, with identifiable faces and bristling whiskers and lost, blind, bumping expressions.

"Moths," says Elliot. "Just moths. I don't believe you, Joanna. You scared me. And all you saw was a few moths. Is that all you saw? Joanna?"

"All? They're disgusting. They have eyes, Elliot. They have faces." Joanna shudders, keeps her eyes on her plate, where the steak, in its small pool of blood and grease is taking on a powdery look, a greyness, the brittle look of something long dead and flightless.

"We're living in the country, Joanna," says Elliot. "This is the country. You can't expect citified little bugs out here, you know." Elliot sits down and takes up his fork. He gives her a frown that's half censure, half amusement and shakes his head. Joanna can tell that he's decided to think of her as cute and girlish: afraid of bugs.

And so she is. She pushes her steak around on her plate, then hides it under her napkin. Later, she will shovel it into the kitchen garbage can.

The sun is rising slowly, slowly above the giant evergreens; long rays of light filter through the branches; forest light: oblique, heavy, the kind of light that nurtures all these hidden, moist growing things: ferns, black twinberry, bunchberry, false bugbane. Joanna sits high up in her window, stitching, basting ruffling tape to slippery brown curtain material, like Snow White's mother.

If the needle should prick Joanna's finger, causing a drop of blood to fall somehow through the glass to the shaded forest floor, would she, in nine months' time, produce a daughter with hair like sunshine, eyes green as moss, lips red as blood? That is what Elliot wants: children. He wants children to fill up the big new house. Sturdy sons, slight-boned daughters, golden-haired.

Perhaps that is what Joanna wants, and perhaps not. Could she produce all those lovely children on order. The thought saddens her. She imagines her name at the bottom of a list: the food processor, the vacuum cleaner, the blender, the electric grill, the convection oven, the fertile womb. Elliot's list.

Consider, just three years from now. Joanna sits at her window stitching and stitching. Patches on tiny overall knees, embroidery on a small white sweater, a thin frill of lace along the edge of a sun bonnet. Below, in a patch of the same peculiar slanted light, Elliot is teaching his small son, his first born, to pedal a shiny new tricycle. See how intently, how lovingly, Elliot's head is bent over the dimpled child. See Elliot's hunched shoulders, strained neck muscles, as he tries and tries to impart the necessary strength and skill to his son. And what is this? An English pram, swathed in mosquito netting, moving gently every now and then on its well-sprung wheels as the babe within kicks and chortles. Elliot's daughter.

How easily this imagined scene could become real, and it is not an unpleasing picture, except in its unrelieved perfection, which makes Joanna run her tongue over her teeth, as if she has eaten candy too rich, too sweet, too cloying for her own good.

There is a stretch of road, at the bottom of their driveway, that is visible from this window, and what should Joanna see there but a young woman, walking. Just strolling by, alone. She is Joanna's age, or younger. She has long hair, loose down her back.

Joanna sits up straight, cranes her neck to see. In over five months no-one has walked past on this road. It is only once in a great while that a car goes past. Joanna wishes herself outside at this moment, working in the small garden Elliot has started. If she was down there mulching the new rhododendrons she could say hello, strike up a conversation. Talk. She could actually talk to someone.

She understands now, what has been wrong all along. She has needed a friend. If she met this girl, she would know someone, someone would know her; she would be real.

Friends, Joanna thinks: we could be friends.

And stabs her needle energetically into the soft brown folds of cloth.

She folds away her sewing and puts the kettle on to boil. She walks quickly up and down the kitchen. A friend, a friend. A beginning. It does cross her mind that she is investing an awful lot of faith in that briefly glimpsed figure, upright and slim though it may be. In those long, even, unhurried steps.

Elliot leaves Joanna with two green-and-white boxes and a new trowel. If she wants to garden, he says, fine. So here she is, cleverly positioned by the road among the young rhododendrons. Elliot has also planted daffodil bulbs. Green spears appear here and there above the peaty soil, and Joanna will bet it is as much in response to Elliot's commands as to the season's urgings.

Joanna takes a shovelful of bone meal, a shovelful of blood meal. The earth is surprisingly cold just beneath the surface. She overturns sleepy earthworms and curled, dormant centipedes. In an undisturbed hollow just beyond their property line, green-skinned skunk cabbages prepare to unfurl their clumsy yellow for spring's indiscriminating sake.

Someone is walking down the road, trotting along in an even measured way. Joanna hears, and digs more vigorously into the damp soil, showering blood meal into the air. She straightens up, and turns at what she considers to be exactly the right moment, so that she can say, in surprise, "Hello!"

She sees at once what is wrong.

It is the same young woman, with the long brown hair, but… Her eyes are tilted in that strange, flat way, rimless and red, watery looking. She has no bridge to her nose, and her face is flat, squished flat. There is no look at all to her thin mouth, but when she smiles, a child's shy smile, Joanna sees the peculiar serrated edges of her small teeth. Joanna can tell that if this girl did not have one chromosome too many, or one too few, she is not sure how it goes, she would have been lovely, with clear blue eyes and milky skin. And all that hair. Poor child, for spring's indiscriminating sake.

"Hello," the girl says, so softly Joanna scarcely hears.

"Hello! Hello, there!" Joanna's voice booms out, false and hearty, a voice she has never, before now, used. "Nice and sunny, isn't it. Warmer," Joanna trills, and the girl nods her head, seriously, consideringly.

"Are you going for a walk?"

"Yes. Now I'm going home." Her voice is level and slow, measured, like her steps, but there is a slight gravelly undertone; like water dragging itself over stones.

"My name is Joanna. What's your name?"

"Fay," she says, and Joanna thinks, well, of course. Fey, fey. Nothing is as it seems here, everything is under a spell, enchanted, witched, upside-down, inside-out. The laws in this land are cold and precise; Joanna thinks she'd do better herself as something wild and green. She tosses her trowel down under a rhododendron and wipes her hands on the back of her jeans.

Fay wears a neat white collar under her coat. Her throat rises from this prim little collar in an exact and hopeful manner. An inch of white cuff shows at each wrist, and she wears a ring: a small amber stone set in gold. When Joanna holds out her hand, it is the hand with the amber ring Fay extends.

"It's nice to meet you, Fay," says Joanna.

"It is nice to meet you," says Fay.

"Listen, would you like to come in? We could have some tea. Milk and cookies?"

Fay looks sideways up at Joanna's tall glass house.

"I have to go home. I have to go right home."

"Is your mother at home? Anyone? We could phone and see if you could stay for a little while."

Fay stares at her feet. Her forehead is bunched up: a white rose.

"No, no. Listen, I know what. Let's both walk to your house. I'll meet your mother, and we'll see if you can visit me at my house soon. Okay?"

They walk down the road together, Joanna in her gardening clothes, her hands smudged with damp earth. She is careful to match her steps to Fay's. Every now and then a cool wind stirs the trees along the road's edge, and Joanna turns her head to receive its chill upon her flushed face.

Fay lives, it turns out, close to the lake front, in a house painted cream with red windowboxes. There are red clay plant pots on the front steps, frilly white curtains at the two front windows. Fay's mother welcomes Joanna in with just the right amount of surprise. She is a tall spare woman with springy grey hair and a gold filling between her large front teeth. She removes a pile of knitting and an old brown teddy bear from a chair so that Joanna can sit down. It is at once obvious to Joanna that this woman sees her interest in Fay as some kind of charitable gesture: a good work. Fay's mother is probably very good at good works: Joanna imagines her rushing from one place to another with washed grapes, old magazines, recycled toys, crocheted potholders. "Of course Fay can visit you, how lovely of you to ask. And how clever of you, Fay, to find this nice lady. We're very isolated here, you know," she says to Joanna, smiling largely with her gold filling.

So Jocelyn, that is her name, Jocelyn, gives her blessing to Joanna. She does not, never would, think of Fay as a friend for Joanna, of Joanna as Fay's friend.

And the next day Fay does indeed walk up Joanna's steep driveway to knock at the door. Joanna has a plate of freshly baked chocolate-chip cookies waiting. Fay kneels on the carpet, content, and moves chess pieces across the coffee-table. March, march goes the king. Scurry, scurry, the queen in his wake. The bishop falls with a soft plop to the floor. Fay picks him up and fondly wipes him clean, scours his mitre with a forefinger. She is lost in play, and does not even bother to watch the television, which Joanna has turned on for her.

Joanna watches, though, with her feet propped up on the edge of the coffee-table; watches the coloured flickers going back and forth. Outside it is raining, the sky is low and dark: comforting. When Joanna was a child she wanted a sister, a baby sister, sweet and malleable. That is Fay. She is like a doll; she smiles and smiles, and sometimes she sits perfectly still.

"Would you like to see the rest of the house, Fay?" Joanna asks suddenly. That is what Elliot always says, very early on, when he has friends to visit. But Fay does not say, as Elliot's friends say, "What a beautiful house." Instead her attention hangs for moments at a time on a deep windowsill, an exposed beam high up against stark whiteness, a cold curve of glass where there should, perhaps, be no glass at all. "Pretty," she says, but with a grave doubt, which Joanna shares. How can any dwelling look so beautiful, and be so cheerless, so comfortless? Joanna and Fay stand with their necks strained back and look up, up, at the high pure angle of wall and ceiling, and Joanna thinks how easily she and Fay could simply disappear, their molecules unlining, thinning, drifting into those odd impossible spaces.

Fay shrugs, and wanders off. She picks up a framed picture of Elliot and butts her finger against the glass. "Your Daddy?"

"No, no, that's Elliot. My husband."

The picture was taken the summer before, on the balcony of their apartment. Elliot is fond of this picture because the camera has given a foreign look, an air of holiday excitement, to the bland local sky. Spain, or the south of France, Italy, it might be, places to which Elliot aspires. Or did aspire, the old Elliot, before he mortgaged his wings.

"Elliot," Fay repeats, and giggles behind her fingers.

"Oh, now, what's so funny?" says Joanna, taking the photograph from Fay. "Elliot isn't so bad."

"He looks like a man on TV."

Joanna wipes the glass in the frame with an edge of her shirt. "He looks like an actor?"

Fay is on her way back to the chess pieces. "No, just like a man on TV," she says.

When Elliot comes home that night he closes the door very quietly behind him. "Do we have any aspirin?" he says. "I have such a headache."

"You aren't the first person I've spoken to all day, for a change," Joanna says, although it couldn't possibly be what she meant to say.

Elliot holds onto his head and looks at her as if she is a

light that hurts his eyes.

"I met someone yesterday. She came over today. Her name is Fay."

"Good. We need to get to know some local people." He kneads the back of his neck, rubs his eyes with his knuckles. "What does her husband do?"

"She's not married," says Joanna. She slams a casserole dish down on the counter, hard. She stares at Elliot, who stands there, bleak and cranky, the corners of his mouth pulled down. Old, dissatisfied, remote, involved entirely with his own selfish pain. That is how Elliot looks to Joanna.

"I'm going to lie down for a while. You go ahead and eat without me." He pauses in the hall by the living-room and calls back, aggrieved, "Joanna, why in God's name is the chess game all over the floor?"

Off limps Elliot, head in hands. Joanna sits on a kitchen stool. It is dusk, and soon after, it is dark. Joanna does not bother to turn on the lights. The chicken breasts in mushroom sauce grow cold; they congeal.

At last she slides off the stool and goes to look at Elliot, who lies with his knees drawn up under the comforter. His face is moonlit, white; his breathing is a soft sigh. This is Elliot's healing sleep, deep as the ocean. When he wakes he will be like a child in the morning, and he will undoubtedly find Joanna, with her vague unhappiness, her demands, pleas, sudden movements, quite incomprehensible. He will begin to wonder if they speak different languages, so difficult is it for him to understand just what she wants.

She lies on the edge of the bed, not disturbing Elliot at all. She lies with her eyes open, staring up at the distant light of the moon, caught in the trapezoid of glass above the mirrored bedroom wall.

"Elliot, I don't think it's working out. Our living here."
Joanna spreads marmalade on toast and passes it to Elliot.
"Living here isn't working out for me, Elliot. I'm alone
here every day. All day long."

"Joanna, please. I would like to enjoy my breakfast."
Elliot gets up, brings a small radio back to the table. He
fiddles with the dial, bites into his toast.

"You have to listen, Elliot. I do not like it here. I can't
live here, Elliot."

"Joanna, give it a chance, will you."

"I have. I have given it a chance." Joanna's voice trem-
bles, she wipes at her nose with the back of her hand.

"Five months?" Elliot pats her hand. "You'll adjust.
You should learn how to drive, Joanna. I'll get you a car."

Joanna shrugs away from him and pours herself another
cup of coffee. After he has left, after he has dropped a care-
less kiss on the top of her head, after he has dismissed *her,*
and left, the words come. Everything she wanted to say.
This is what I miss, Elliot, she tells him in her mind:
sidewalks, warmed by the sun. Little bits of chocolate-
bar wrapper rolling past in the breeze, faces, smiling, not
smiling, so much variety, so much humanity. Dusty
awnings above the greengrocers, bunches of cut flowers,
89¢ each, in dented metal buckets. Flocks of schoolchil-
dren in blue serge uniforms playing hopscotch in front of
the red-brick Catholic school. Flocks of pigeons. The
city, Elliot. The city.

Elliot, her imaginary Elliot, leans forward, clearly
intrigued. She has caught his attention. But wait. Elliot
is not, will not be convinced. He is amused by all the
obvious things she has left out of her pretty picture, some
of which he lists off for her, counting on his fingers: street
muggings, pollution, high rent, pigeon mites, noise,
drunks in their grimy sleeps on park benches, in gutters;
graft in City Hall. Now there are bars in front of Elliot's

131

smug face. Thin, looped iron, a priest's confessional. In a minute he will draw a thick, short curtain over the bars. He will vanish. First: "Joanna, you are not consistent. And as for logic! Why, you present the city as a fairy-tale world, all sunshine. Then you expect me to believe that you're afraid and unhappy in our beautiful new house. Joanna! You're not being reasonable. You're not giving yourself time. You need time, Joanna."

Elliot is not a priest, he is a crow, holding his wings tight against his sleek body. He is a crow and he speaks a different language from Joanna indeed.

Joanna throws the breakfast dishes into the sink and wipes toast crumbs off the table onto the floor. She goes to the telephone and calls Jocelyn, who chirps and sings like a finch at the idea of Fay having dinner with Joanna and her husband. "How extremely kind of you, dear," she tells Joanna. "Fay has led a very protected life, I'm afraid. Very protected, and rather isolated. This will be just lovely for her."

Fay is dressed for a party, dressed for a celebration, dressed in taffeta, stiff and rustling, the colour of unpolished brass. Her mother's best dress, 30 years old, with the folds shaken out, Joanna suspects, but still Fay looks young and doll-like, her neck and shoulders rise tenderly out of the exotic foliage, she is not at all spoilt by such tawdry coverings.

Joanna brushes Fay's long hair, sprays perfume on her neck. Fay shivers and laughs noisily, moistly, through her small bridgeless nose; laughs and points at the mirror, curtsies clownishly. Joanna stands beside her; together, they bow at the mirror.

The kitchen is hot and steamy. Joanna has overdone things a little. Fat splatters against the oven walls; water from a pot sizzles on the stove-top.

Soon Elliot will come home, he will walk into the kitchen, he will see that someone is here. He will see Fay.

What exactly is she trying to prove here? That is what Elliot will want to know. Oh, he'll go right to the heart of the matter and accuse her. He'll say she is using Fay. He'll say she wants him to think that the only friend she has is a retarded girl. But Fay is her friend. And what harm, in any case? What harm?

"Here, you slice the tomatoes for the salad, Fay." Joanna gives her the knife. "You must be careful though. Be careful not to cut yourself."

Fay bends over her task. Her hands move slowly, slowly. The tomato bleeds into the cutting-board.

"And candles," says Joanna brightly. "Let's have lots of candles for a pretty light." The candelabrum, and five crystal candle holders. Joanna strikes a match. Outside, the garage door slams shut.

She knows Elliot; she should know Elliot by now. But she doesn't. He is always one step ahead of her. There is no change of expression, nothing to watch, nothing she wouldn't see when he meets anyone for the first time.

"Ah, you're Joanna's friend. Fay. How do you do. Well, this is quite a party. Joanna, my love, you should have told me."

Fay is overcome: the man on TV in real life. She smiles shyly up at Elliot and bites at the side of her finger; her amber ring sparkles in the candlelight.

"My, it smells good in here," says Elliot. "We must be having my favourite, roast moose."

Fay chuckles. She stands with the knife in one hand, a tomato in the other. "Not roast moose."

"Well then, roast hippopotamus?"

"No!"

"Roast dinosaur?"

133

Fay is scarlet with laughter. "No, no, no," she says, and drops the knife to the floor.

"Stop it Elliot," Joanna says. She picks the knife up and smiles. "Stop it."

"It's roast beef then, I suppose. Well, you should have told me, Joanna. I would have been prepared. If you'd told me I was having roast beef for supper, I would have been prepared for roast beef. I wouldn't have expected something quite different. I wonder why Joanna always leaves me guessing, don't you wonder, Fay? I think I'll give up trying to second guess old Joanna. Well, shall I carve the roast beef, Joanna? Does it matter to you how I slice it?"

"Not a bit," says Joanna. She undoes Fay's apron and leads her to the table.

Three for dinner. Mummy and Daddy and baby makes three. Joanna spears a potato, brings it slowly to her lips. The flames from the candles, ten flames, leave blue and green after-images on the retinas of her eyes. "Would you like some more water, Fay? Or some milk?"

"Milk, please," says Fay quietly. She has gone very quiet, aware, probably, that something is askew in the room, something is wrong between Joanna and the man. She smooths at her taffeta skirt under the table.

"You grew up around here?" Elliot moves a candle half an inch, so that he can talk to Fay. "You live close to us?"

"Yes. My house is by the lake. It has a red roof."

"By the lake. You go swimming there?"

"In the summer. When it's hot." Fay grins. "My dog swims in the winter, too, though."

"He doesn't mind the cold water?"

"He doesn't care. He's just a dog."

"You like living by the lake. Yes, it must be nice. Joanna wouldn't like it, but then Joanna doesn't like anything very much. Do you, Joanna love?"

"I think I'll get dessert," says Joanna.

In the kitchen Joanna leans her forehead against the fridge door. Hot and cool. Everything is going wrong. She has to find the little gold dessert forks; Fay will think they are pretty. They were a wedding present, never used. They are in a box somewhere, a box with white satin lining. Not where she thought they were, not in the next three places she looks, but on the top shelf of a cupboard over the stove. Joanna wipes them carefully with a soft cloth, sets them down on a tray beside the dessert plates, beside the wedges of lemon meringue pie.

Candlelight is going wild: shadows bend wildly on the dark walls. Joanna sees why at once and hurries to put the tray down on the table. "No, Fay. No," she cries. Then she says, in a voice meant to sound reasonable, reasonable and calm: "Please don't open that window Fay," but Fay has already pushed the window wide, one foot out behind her for balance, like a dancer.

"It's hot in here," says Elliot, conversationally. Reaching across the table for his coffee. "Hot and muggy."

The moths appear as if they emerged from Elliot's mouth, as if they were blown softly from his mouth, like bubbles. They fly to the candlelight, of course, dusty brown bombers, trekking across the room, fixed, blind, lusting terribly for Joanna's pretty candle flames.

They seem big as bats to Joanna: big and wilful, especially the one, or two, that brush against her arms, that flap dry wings against her skin, against her hair.

Elliot grabs her by the wrists. She cannot move her arms. "Stop that, Joanna," he says, as if he is upset by the way she is hitting out. "They're only moths. Only moths." He nods his head toward a corner of the room, the corner where the window meets the wall. Fay is there, with her knuckles in her mouth, her eyes huge: a misbehaving child.

"You're frightening her," Elliot says.

Fay removes her fists from her mouth. "I am not frightened," she says. Her eyes move quickly, searching out the room: they shimmer. And, unaccountably, she smiles.

Joanna almost misses the movement, it is so quick, but suddenly Fay is in front of her. She is radiant, lit from within. She holds her cupped hands up. "I have one," she says, simply.

Joanna shakes her head; no. But it is difficult for her to protest, to say anything at all. She is confronted with this young saint in taffeta. An image, a likeness—of what? For a moment Joanna is drawn irresistibly to Fay, and even lifts her own hands to place them over Fay's, but Fay's hands are slowly opening. Joanna pulls back to avoid the dreadful revelation.

The moth does not fly as soon as the hands open: perhaps it is under the same spell Joanna felt. It shuffles to the top of Fay's finger and perches there, a particularly fine and vigorous specimen, tentatively passing its hooked feet in front of its shuttered eyes.

"See," says Fay, with a small, tight laugh. "You don't have to be frightened. It can't hurt you." She moves her hand forward, to give Joanna a better look.

"I don't want to see it, Fay. Stop that."

"It's pretty. It tickles," Fay says softly. The moth flutters its wings, only inches from Joanna's face.

"I was scared, at first," Fay offers.

"You're too stupid to be scared," Joanna says, and after the first shock her words cause, she goes on: "You're an idiot, Fay. Stupid, stupid. You are."

"Joanna, stop," Elliot hisses into her ear. "What is it you want here, Joanna?" He places the palm of his hand on her back and gives her a little shove. "Go into the bedroom. Lie down. I'll take care of this."

She listens from the bedroom door, supporting herself against the wall. Elliot is comforting Fay; his voice, soft, low, soothing, goes on and on. There is another sound: perhaps Fay is crying.

In a while she hears footsteps, doors closing. The car moves down the long drive onto the road. Joanna hears tires bite into gravel, sees briefly reflected ribbons of light cross the walls and ceiling of her room, and then she is alone.

I Pay My Rent?

W. P. Kinsella

I have lived in this massive, old frame house for four years. Only Gabon has been here longer. The house leans at odd, erotic angles. I'm still not sure that I've been in all the rooms and apartments. Multiple additions have been built on over the many years since the house was new. Some owner, desperate for money, rented a sun-porch or pantry, and built on a new sun-porch or pantry, which was later rented out by a subsequent owner. Years ago the double garage was converted to an apartment. Later, a room was added on top of the garage, then still another room was piled on top of that.

A Mrs. Kryzanowski owns the property now, inherited from her husband, a hollow-cheeked, cancerous-looking man who cashed in his pale soul soon after I arrived four years ago. He had purchased the house from the estate of an elderly Chinese, who had died in one of the sun-porches amid stacks of Chinese newspapers and three bamboo cages filled with thimble-sized canaries.

Before the Chinese, history blurs.

Gabon lives in the attic above the third floor. He occupies a tiny loft with one dark, triangular window that overlooks the back alley. The attic is reached by pulling down a black metal ladder, which hugs the ceiling like a long, wrought-iron spider, and climbing through a trap door.

I'm sure Gabon's presence in the attic must violate thousands of fire and building-code regulations, but none of us are about to call in outsiders, who, in order to *protect* us, would evict us. The rent is cheap; the house is warm, and each of us lives with our own secrets, which may be as frayed as a favourite blanket or as vicious as a Tasmanian devil.

Gabon is small and brown with bird-like ankles and wrists; his nose is hooked and black tufts of hair bristle from his head at odd angles. I knew someone from Sumatra who looked like him: tiny, starved-looking, cinnamon-skinned. There is a sour, bachelor smell about Gabon, of unemptied ashtrays and soiled clothing.

Whenever I meet him on the sidewalk or in the halls he nods shyly.

"I pay my rent," he informs me, speaking in a sibilant whisper, his accent unidentifiable: Spanish? Greek? Arabic of some ilk? I suspect he knows only two English phrases: "Nice day," offered even when it is raining torrentially, and "I pay my rent." The latter is delivered as if he is asking a question like "How are you?"

The phrase must have impressed Mrs. Kryzanowski, for when I say, after counting twenty-dollar bills into her bluish hand, "Tell me about Gabon?" she replies, "He pays his rent." The expression on her pink, naughahide face lets me know unequivocally that Gabon is a good tenant and that she would be happier if I paid my rent on time more often and asked fewer questions.

"I pay my rent too," I say, trying to smile disarmingly.

"Sometimes," says Mrs. Kryzanowski.

But I refuse to be dismissed so easily. I stand leaning on the door-jamb, waiting. Mrs. Kryzanowski is wearing a ghastly flowered housecoat; her white hair has incongruous lemon streaks in it and is wound around candy-apple-blue rollers. Her face is paved with makeup that may well have been applied with a palette-knife.

"Noisy, noisy," she finally says. "A jockey. Broked his neck once," and she makes a cracking motion with her large hands, like snapping invisible kindling.

"Noisy?"

"Walk, walk, walk. Ax-ersize maybe? Who knows. Everybody's crazy over there."

Mrs. Kryzanowski lives two blocks away in a one-storey, basement-less house with unlevel floors covered in bulging linoleum. She never visits the "Castle" as our rooming-house is referred to by residents and neighbours alike.

"He has a *doght*," she volunteers, smiling conspiratorily. He tinks I don't know."

Mrs. Kryzanowski obviously has a spy at the Castle. It is probably Grabarkewitcz, who lives in a room below me in the company of a magical cat. Mrs. Kryzanowski had Grabarkewitcz' room painted last month, the only maintenance she has authorized since she has owned the Castle.

A dog. Interesting.

Night and day, I frequently haunt the halls of the Castle, inhaling the odours of varnish, cooked cabbage, mothballs and dust. Mrs. Kryzanowski harbours quite a genteel collection of loners and losers. Tenants who disturb the status quo are dealt with swiftly. Last summer a stringy-haired thug rented a first-floor room and soon had it swarming with beer-swilling friends who argued, fought, played a tinny radio at full volume and urinated out the window into Mrs. Kryzanowski's caragana hedge.

One afternoon a lithe oriental with steel-coloured hair and bitter eyes called on the thug and his friends. The caller was verbally abused and threatened. The young oriental bowed curtly as the door was slammed in his face.

The next time the thug exited by the side door, there was one sharp bleat of pain, brief scuffling in the caragana, then silence. Late that evening the thug moved, his thug friends carrying his few possessions. The thug carried only a few soiled clothes crushed to his body with his left arm. His right arm bore a blazing white cast, resting like an angel in a clean, white sling.

I knew how Gabon reached his living quarters but had never seen the deed accomplished. Like most of us here Gabon had no employment and kept irregular hours. I lurked behind my curtains for two days before I spied Gabon approaching the house. I huffed up two flights of stairs and down a long corridor. I was loitering beneath the black ladder when Gabon arrived.

"Evening," I said.

"Nice day," said Gabon; he was clutching an apple in his right hand.

"It is," I said. It was.

"I pay my rent," said Gabon, again treating the statement as a question. Perhaps he had been misled by a deceitful English-as-a-second-language instructor.

Gabon nervously forced the apple into a side pocket, then flexing his knees sprang straight into the air and grabbed the bottom rung of the ladder with both hands. There was barely enough of Gabon, 90 pounds would be my guess, to pull the ladder down until the bottom rung was a foot from the floor. When the ladder was in position he scampered up the eight or so rungs, quickly, like a native scaling a palm tree, and pushed open the trap door to the attic. He disappeared like a burglar and the ladder swung eerily back into place emitting a few soft, metal groans.

I remained in the dim hall for a long time. Gabon did pace about a great deal, sometimes seeming to break into a run. He also seemed to be talking to someone, though the words were indistinguishable, and could have come from a radio.

He must have been uneasy about his encounter with me for after about twenty minutes the trap door creaked open and Gabon hung his head down and peered furtively around. I was pressed against the wall at the head of the stairs, out of view.

Back in my room I open the window and crawl out onto the porch roof below me; I crawl about twenty feet where, when I carefully stand up, at about shoulder height is another addition to the Castle. By pulling myself up and over two more portions of the building, and risking great embarrassment and multiple fractures, I am able to climb onto the roof of Gabon's loft. I slither forward to the very peak of the roof, and by hanging precariously over the edge, am able to peer into Gabon's triangular window. It is a crisp October night and I am silvered by the moon as I hang grotesquely, like a broken TV antennae.

In the loft, which is lit by the yellowish light from one 60-watt bulb, sits Gabon, not on a chair or bed, but on the back of a small, shaggy, brown-and-white pony.

Gabon, no larger than a ten-year-old, is dressed in jockey silks of parrot-green and ivory, a white-and-green jockey's cap on his head, goggles resting on the crown of the cap.

The pony is a bit over three feet tall, Gabon sits on a scaled-down racing saddle, it and his tall boots polished to the colour of gleaming liver.

In one corner of the loft is Gabon's pallet. In the other, cordoned off by small packing-crates, is straw for bedding and grass for eating. Gabon rides the pony in a slow circle; the middle of the room is covered in brown indoor-outdoor carpet. The pony prances. Gabon waves to the crowd.

I try to imagine Gabon smuggling the pony into the loft. It is too big to remove now, but I suppose as a colt it would have been no larger than a full-grown spaniel.

Now, on this brilliant October night, in one of the loneliest places on earth, Gabon parades around the winner's circle under the blazing sun of Hialeah, Pimlico or Churchill Downs, accepting his accolades, remembering the clash of the starting gate, the yelp of the crowds as his horse lunged forward, sleek, powerful, pliant as butter between his thighs.

Avis de Vente

Joyce Marshall

Did we have drought in the east too in those years? The
day comes back to me as tense, almost crackling with dry-
ness, gritty. Of course, now that we were to be year-
round people instead of merely summer people, we lived
far from the water. (There was no blurring of boundaries
in that community of, at most, three hundred people—
French in the village proper, rich English on an upthrust
of land called The Heights, ordinary English on a few little streets between The Heights and the village, summer
English on a reedy stretch by the lake, which wasn't really

lake, just a swelling and slowing of the Ottawa River, a catch-basin for shadflies, always rather smelly as summer waned.) Our house, a white-painted wooden structure with what was known in Quebec as a gallery around three sides, was about as far from the pseudo-lake and its coolness as it could be—the last house on the last of the three or four ordinary English streets.

There must have been a strange shabby man being fed on the gallery when I came down. There was most mornings and it seems to me that I could hear a blur of solemn adult voices as I settled with my bowl of cereal on the front steps. Though my mother had been moody and short-tempered since we moved out from Montreal with our furniture in April, soon after my baby brother was born, she always sat and talked to these men. "Isn't it terrible!" I remember her saying once. "A man like that who was all through The War!" For though they slept in the rough stretch of bush just above our house, these men weren't tramps. They were "the unemployed" and were on their way from Montreal to Ottawa or from Ottawa to Montreal to look for work. I can't recall anything about that morning's visitor, just that vague sense of adult voices in the background as I crouched with my cornflakes on the front steps. Brooding as usual was the way my mother would have put it. (And probably did. She did most mornings.) I wasn't brooding. I was thinking. About my best friend Alison, whose family were also going to be year-round people, in a house just a field away from ours. And about myself. I was much on my mind at that time. The adolescence that seemed to be whirling Alison away from me was turning me secretive and dark. Unpredictable, even to myself. Alison had gone in to Montreal to see Gary Cooper in *Wings,* which she'd already seen three times. I hadn't seen it even once. Though Alison was still too young to enter a movie thea-

145

tre legally—Quebec had many strange restrictive statutes in those days—she easily passed for sixteen. I was thirteen, just a year and three months younger, but the one time she'd coached me in grown-up behaviour so I could sneak in beside her, I'd been challenged. I badly wanted to see Gary Cooper, to find out whether I too would shiver and weep as Alison claimed she did. That's what I was thinking in the dry sun of that early morning. That's all I was thinking. Till it occurred to me that if I plotted very carefully, and didn't lose my nerve at the last, I might be able to use Alison's absence as an excuse to stay home alone that afternoon.

My mother didn't encourage solitude in her children, especially not solitude in an empty house. Not that she feared that anything might happen to us. A desire to be alone at times was just one of many things she found perverse about me. My differences with my mother go back to a country I cannot enter now; emotions are sharp and savage there, my sense of right and wrong absolute and strict. I was fighting, whether I knew it or not, for my life—or at least for some sense of a self I could glimpse only briefly now and then, might not have recognized as mine if I could have seen it clear and whole. Meanwhile I simply fought, with shrieks and insults, about everything. "Why aren't you more like other people?" she used to say. "Why don't you want to go out and have a little fun?" Which wasn't fair, because most of the time I was quite willing to go out and have fun, even the sort of fun Alison wanted us to have this year—splashing about, as close to the big boys as we could get, instead of properly swimming, or pacing the main street of the village in our best clothes when there were so many more interesting things to do, like breaking into unused summer cottages. Every now and then, however, I liked the idea of being alone in our house, with no-one rushing in or audible in another room, so I could work on one of the long stories I was writing at that time, or read, or get my diary out from the hiding-place I changed each day or two to fool my sisters.

We did gardening chores after breakfast, I imagine. My father had dug a huge plot this year—it was part of the fun, he said, of being year-round people instead of just transient summer people—and though in the past he'd often helped us dig up seeds to check on their sprouting, gardening was serious business now. We spent far too much time, we thought, hoeing or weeding or scratching our wrists in the raspberry patch.

It was a Saturday so he came home with the other fathers on the noon train. We still had fathers in those days and as far as we knew we would always have them. (I am amazed sometimes that we could have lived unknowing among so many who were doomed—to the car in the closed garage, the numbing whisky drunk in the slowly warming snow, the blood vessel bursting, flooding the brain with ice.) I liked our house very much better when my father was in it. Liked myself better too. He seemed to find me less strange than my mother did and so I became less strange. But how do you explain love? Should you try even? I still find after all this time that I don't want to examine it too closely, don't want to find at the last that he's written away and gone. I'll just say that he was lively and filled all spaces. He could keep us entertained for hours, telling long stories in Anglican plainchant or drawing exotically feathered chickens, one after the other, scarcely looking at what he was doing. Above all he sang, from the moment he woke up—in church choirs, in amateur operas and operettas, all over our house, on the street.

I suppose we made our usual sandwiches and ate them wherever we chose and that there was the usual flurry of getting my father off to play tennis—helping him search for his tennis racket, gathering a supply of the big white handkerchiefs he knotted at the corners to make little hats. I'd like to linger here, hang onto the last of the ordinary part of that day. But there is never a clanging of bells. I can't remember whether Hilary took Claudia or whether Laura took her. All three went off to swim. I know that much. I sat on the front steps and watched them go with their bathing caps and towels. Last of all, my mother bundled the baby into his carriage and wheeled him out. I was waiting for Alison, I told her. She had an errand for her mother and would signal me when she got back. Though I still didn't look at her much, I forced myself to do it now. (I'd been too embarrassed during her pregnancy, which hadn't been explained to me and which I'd been expected neither to notice nor comprehend. I was embarrassed still by her habit of acting like a young cooing mother with the baby, when she must be over 40, though she would never tell us her age.) She simply nodded at my words, on her face the absent look it so often wore these days. My mother had many such looks—just before she set off for one of her long solitary swims in the deep water, often when you came into a room and found her there alone. But is "absent" with its suggestion of inwardness, even blindness, the right word? My mother's eyes, which were a brighter brown than anyone else's, blazed at these away times. They saw. Something. I hadn't yet begun to wonder what this was.

I watched her go down the walk, already singing to the baby, then went into the house. I'd be in trouble later, I knew, for telling what my mother called "a story." She never said "lie." "Don't tell stories" was how she put it —a babyish admonition that offended me. This was certainly a story if there ever was one and it was going to get me a good three or four hours of just being alone in our house.

The living-room was dim—green-dim. My mother had closed the slatted wooden shutters that used to be hooked onto Quebec houses the day the double windows came down. They were heavy, often poorly fitted, inclined to bang in any sort of wind, but on still days they washed a room with green. I wandered around for a while, noticing how strange our city furniture looked in these different spaces and quite on its own, trying to decide what I would do. This always took time since I could never be sure till the last that one of my schemes for being alone would work. I'd just brought down my current story and was so absorbed in the problems of Robinette, a rich beautiful girl with several suitors—should she marry her guardian, who was just a little older than she was but limped badly (most of my heroines did eventually marry their guardians) or the young doctor who took her sailing and skiing?—that I didn't hear the car, steps on the walk or the gallery, anything in fact until the knock.

To my surprise, for I knew everyone in our community (except "the unemployed" and they always came much earlier to the back of the house), the man I could see through the screen door was a stranger—a short, broad, extremely serious stranger, dressed in what I thought of as city clothes. Most French Canadians did wear city clothes in those days; even the farmers, from that vague region up beyond the bush known as the back country, put on hats and sober suits to sell eggs. It was one of the many things that were different about them. They didn't swim or play tennis and though darker the rest of the time, in summer they were paler than we were.

He asked for my father. I said he was out. Then for my mother. I said she was also out. He thrust a paper into my hands, saying he'd just come in then and mark a few things down in a list. It was the gravity more than his words that panicked me. I thrust the paper back at him. I couldn't read it, I said, it was in French. I could read the only three words I'd looked at, *Avis de Vente* in heavy print across the top, had seen them in all sorts of places—*Avis* notice, *Vente* sale. I was alone in the house, I told him. I was forbidden to let a strange man into the house with me when I was alone. To make my words more emphatic, I put a hand on either side of the doorway. I felt like Madeleine de Verchères at least. I'd always admired Madeleine, the one heroic girl I'd encountered in history.

He looked at me, a man with a mean little job who'd get into trouble probably if he came back with the tale of finding no-one home but a thirteen-year-old girl and she'd refused to let him in. Perhaps I was too young. I wonder now whether he was quite sure about this as he stood there and repeated that all he wanted to do was mark a few things down in a list. I didn't believe him. I thought our household goods would be removed forthwith for the sale referred to on the paper. He must finally have realized this for his manner changed. He wasn't a moving-company, he said. Did that look like a truck? indicating his dust-covered car by the gate. Surely a smart little lady like I was could see that he wasn't Baillargeon or any of the other big movers from Montreal, he added with the sort of belittling jokiness children catch at once because they've known it all their lives. He just wanted to mark a few things down in a list, he repeated. When my father came home, I'd give him the paper. He'd have several days to pay up. He showed me the figure. I've forgotten it now but, as I remember, it wasn't large. "In fact," he said, "I'll tell you something I maybe shouldn't because I can see that you're a smart young lady. He doesn't have to pay the whole shot. He just puts down a few dollars and it's fixed. Let me in. I won't take anything. I won't hurt you." I continued in my dramatics for a few minutes more but the humour told me I was lost. (The Iroquois hadn't been able to make silly grown-up jokes with Madeleine. She'd had a gun or two, been secure behind a palisade.) I sensed that he wouldn't push me aside as he could quite easily have done. He'd just stand there teasing me till the rest of the family came home. So I withdrew my hands from the door-frame and let him in.

At once he became businesslike. He glanced at, and discarded, the chairs and chesterfield in the living-room and walked through to the dining-room, where he marked down the table but not the chairs—or at least not the side chairs which, because of a family habit of teetering, had been glued back together several times. He did mark down the heavy armchair in which my father sat, the serving-table, the sideboard.

I couldn't stop being dramatic even now. "Why don't you mark down the cut-glass bowls?" I asked him. "Why don't you mark down this doll of my sister's? Why don't you mark down the kiddy car?"

He was smiling as he went back to the living-room, saw the roll-top desk under one of the windows and marked that down. He then handed me a copy of the paper, with the list, reminding me that I must give it to my father, tipped his hat, said he hoped he hadn't disturbed me too much, and left. I stood in the doorway, watching as dust from that un-oiled country road billowed up behind his car and hung there, loosening slowly.

I read the notice through and understood all of it except some law-terms in a queer mixed language that would have been dark to me even in English. The bill was for stationery supplies and printing. The sum, as I said, wasn't large. (My father sold something known throughout our childhood as stocksandbonds. He'd had, perhaps at the time still had, an office on St. James Street.) I put the paper under my pillow and sat on one of the rejected chairs, pale rose-coloured once, much of its pattern now soiled and rubbed away. I picked up my story and put it down again. Though I had four new library books, I didn't feel like reading. I didn't even think of confiding the matter to my diary. I never did, as it happened. That is the trouble with this incident. Though I talk a great deal about my childhood—writers have more childhood than other people or perhaps they just carry more of it with them—I've never mentioned it to anyone. It remains—unshaped, unsoftened, unabsorbed. I should be able to pull it out whole but it resists—a burr in the past and in my flesh. I must have been aware of things and incidents I'd been too caught up in my own adolescence to examine slipping into place. I remember only numbness and the green dimness of that cool dry living-room. I sat, scarcely moving, till I heard my mother on the walk, then ran upstairs and put the paper for greater safety under the bottom sheet of my bed.

I was back in the big chair by the time my mother came in. She was singing to the baby again in that silly way; her face still wore its away look—as if, I thought, the look belonged to one person, the singing to another. I'd have liked a real row, for her to give me a good tongue-lashing about my disgraceful habit of telling stories, but all she said when she saw me was that it was a pity for a little girl to be so dependent upon a particular friend that she wasted a whole beautiful summer day waiting for that friend. Moping about with her head in a book. I wanted to scream at her that I hadn't been reading. Why was she always picking on me? Why wouldn't she ever let me do anything I wanted to do? I couldn't. So, she continued, dumping the baby in my lap, suppose I made myself useful for a change by entertaining her darling while she saw about supper.

I blew on the baby's eyelids to make him laugh. He

smelled as he always did, fresh and innocent, like grass. Hilary wandered home a little later, then Laura, and they were put to work setting the table. I snuffled the baby's hair, listening to them talking to one another, as we all did that summer, in a sort of imitation French—our notion of a French accent and occasional words or even phrases learned at school. They were compact, easy children, or so I thought, for I'd always assumed that they knew things I might never know, had been born knowing these things. They seemed very far away, moving so innocently around that table, their own untroubled selves. Last of all came my father with Claudia on his shoulder. Claudia had been the baby longer than any of the rest of us—almost five years. Her nose was still out of joint because of the usurper, the new baby, so my father was being particularly attentive to her. He waited till she'd finished the story she was telling him—Claudia had the gift of almost total recall at that time and insisted upon recounting, with gulps, in one long sentence, all the stories that were read to her—then went upstairs. I set the baby in his pen and followed, and when he came out of the bathroom, hair and face dripping, I handed him the paper.

He glanced at it, said, "Oh well yes" in a strange, I thought angry voice, then turned away.

I'd been looking at him so intently, waiting for him to explain it all, make everything right, that I'd seen everything that happened to his face. His eyes, which were a clear blue-grey though his hair and skin were dark, had held an expression I'd never expected to see in my father's eyes. Did I name it then? Did I recognize uncertainty and shame? I began to speak wildly, sharply. I'd hidden the paper, I said, because I didn't want Mother to see it, Mother was in such a crabby mood these days, and it wasn't as bad as it sounded, he'd just have to put down a few—

"What was that?" my father said in that same, I thought angry voice.

"Nothing," I said and went into my room.

The Depression is spoken of as a time of comradeship. People were together in those years, they were generous with what little they had. What we leave out, and I am as bad as anyone, is the shame. People weren't really together. They hid—as individuals, as families. Children were "spared." Even after they came to know the worst, they had to pretend they didn't know. We Depression children grew up early, if growing up meant seeing our parents to some extent at least as individuals apart from ourselves. Some of us even learned to spare our parents. Not soon or well enough, for three or four years after that summer day came the time I always think of as The Death of Fathers—three out of that small community in cars in their garage, a fourth in a snowdrift on one of the sideroads far up in the back country. (That was my friend Alison's father. He wasn't found for ten days.) My own father was eating lunch in a restaurant in Montreal when he dropped his fork and slipped sideways to the floor. He was bundled into a taxi and would not tell the driver where he lived or be taken to a hospital till $25 and most of his life was gone.

His was my first death (except for a boy-uncle who died when I could understand absence but not death) and as I could not stop expecting his voice or his step, I told myself I had to go back through my memories and write over each of them: my father who was to die. So though he was a gay, laughing and loving person right to the last, all my recollections of him have a little tinge of sadness. My mother sometimes jumps into my mind as alive as she ever was, capricious, fiery, troubling, but moving and changing as the living do. I succeeded too well with my father and I regret this. He doesn't deserve to trail through my mind and memory the same always, marked for early death.

That was one of our liveliest suppers. My mother said, as she did so often, that she couldn't imagine why she bothered to put food on the table for people who kept getting up and running about. My father teased her. She enjoyed it as much as anyone, he said; she just didn't want to admit it. My mother tossed her head and looked angry, smiled—smiled and looked angry at once, which outraged me. Claudia told one of her long stories. Then my father and Hilary sang a duet from Carmen, with English words they made up as they went along. I don't know whether he looked at me in any special way. I was afraid to look at him. I'd been wrong, I knew. He was the father and I was the child. There were lines, I realized, at least I think I realized, that shouldn't be crossed, that he couldn't let be crossed. I knew our furniture wouldn't be sold, he'd put down a few dollars, as the bailiff's man had suggested. The matter would be fixed. Out of my sight. Many things would happen now that concerned me and I would have to pretend I didn't know. I may even have sensed as I sat there listening to the singing that the only way I could spare myself was to spare him. I couldn't love a flawed object at that time; I was too afraid of losing love if my own weren't complete.

I do know that I was rather quiet that evening. I often was so that wasn't remarkable in itself. But at some point, though I was the poorest singer in the family, I added a bit of a verse to the song my father and Hilary were singing. At least I believe I did. I hope I did.

Dog Attempts to Drown Man in Saskatoon

Douglas Glover

My wife and I decide to separate, and then suddenly we are almost happy together. The pathos of our situation, our private and unique tragedy, lends romance to each small act. We see everything in the round, the facets as opposed to the flat banality that was wedging us apart. When she asks me to go to the Mendel Art Gallery Sunday afternoon, I do not say no with the usual mounting irritation that drives me into myself. I say yes and some hardness within me seems to melt into a pleasant sadness. We look into each other's eyes and realize with a start that we are looking for the first time because it is the last. We are both thinking, "Who is this person to whom I have been married? What has been the meaning of our relationship?" These are questions we have never asked ourselves; we have been a blind couple groping with each other in the dark. Instead of saying to myself, "Not the art gallery again! What does she care about art? She has no education. She's merely bored and on Sunday afternoon in Saskatoon the only place you can go is the old sausage-maker's mausoleum of art!" instead of putting up arguments, I think, "Poor Lucy, pursued by the assassins of her past, unable to be still. Perhaps if I had her memories I also would be unable to stay in on a Sunday afternoon." Somewhere that cretin Pascal says that all our problems stem from not being able to sit quietly in a room alone. If Pascal had had Lucy's mother, he would never have written anything so foolish. Also, at the age of nine, she saw her younger brother run over and killed by a highway roller. Faced with that, would Pascal have written anything? (Now I am defending my wife against Pascal! A month ago I would have used the same passage to bludgeon her.)

Note. Already this is not the story I wanted to tell. That is buried, gone, lost—its action fragmented and distorted by inexact recollection. Directly it was completed, it had disappeared, gone with the past into that strange realm of suspended animation, that coat-rack of despair, wherein all our completed acts await, gathering dust, until we come for them again. I am trying to give you the truth, though I could try harder, only refrain because I know that that way leads to madness. So I offer an approximation, a shadow play, such as would excite children, full of blind spots and irrelevant adumbrations, too little in parts; elsewhere too much. Alternately I will frustrate you

157

and lead you astray. I can only say that, at the outset, my intention was otherwise; I sought only clarity and simple conclusions. Now I know the worst!—that reasons are out of joint with actions, that my best explanation will be obscure, subtle and unsatisfying, and that the human mind is a tangle of unexplored pathways.

"My wife and I decide to separate, and then suddenly we are almost happy together." This is a sentence full of ironies and lies. For example, I call her my wife. Technically this is true. But now that I am leaving, the thought is in both our hearts: "Can a marriage of eleven months really be called a marriage?" Moreover, it was only a civil ceremony, a ten-minute formality performed at the City Hall by a man who, one could tell, had been drinking heavily over lunch. Perhaps if we had done it in a cathedral surrounded by robed priests intoning Latin benedictions we would not now be falling apart. As we put on our coats to go to the art gallery, I mention this idea to Lucy. "A year," she says. "With Latin we might have lasted a year." We laugh. This is the most courageous statement she has made since we became aware of our defeat, better than all her sour tears. Usually she is too self-conscious to make jokes. Seeing me smile, she blushes and becomes confused, happy to have pleased me, happy to be happy, in the final analysis, happy to be sad because the sadness frees her to be what she could never be before. Like many people, we are both masters of beginnings and endings but founder in the middle of things. It takes a wise and mature individual to manage that which intervenes, the duration which is a necessary part of life and marriage. So there is a sense in which we are not married, though something *is* ending. And therein lies the greater irony. For in ending, in separating, we are finally and ineluctably together, locked as it were in a ritual recantation. We are going to the art gallery (I am guilty of over-determining the symbol) together.

It is winter in Saskatoon, to my mind the best of seasons because it is the most inimical to human existence. The weather forecaster gives the temperature, the wind-chill factor and the number of seconds it takes to freeze exposed skin. Driving between towns one remembers to pack a winter survival kit (matches, candle, chocolate, flares, down sleeping-bag) in case of a breakdown. Earlier in the week just outside the city limits a man disappeared after setting out to walk a quarter of a mile from one farmhouse to another, swallowed up by the cold prairie night. (This is, I believe, a not unpleasant way to die once the initial period of discomfort has been passed.) Summer in Saskatoon is a collection of minor irritants: heat and dust, blackflies and tent caterpillars, the night-time electrical storms that leave the unpaved concession roads impassable troughs of gumbo mud. But winter has the beauty of a plausible finality. I drive out to the airport early in the morning to watch jets land in a pink haze of ice crystals. During the long nights the *aurora borealis* seems to touch the rooftops. But best of all is the city itself, which takes on a kind of ghostliness, a dreamlike quality that combines emptiness (there seem to be so few people) and the mists rising from the heated buildings to produce a mystery. Daily I tramp the paths along the riverbank, crossing and re-crossing the bridges, watching the way the city changes in the pale winter light. Beneath me the unfrozen parts of the river smoke and boil, raging to become still. Winter in Saskatoon is a time of anxious waiting and endurance; all that beauty is alien, a constant threat. Many things do not endure. Our marriage, for example, was vernal, a product of the brief, sweet, prairie spring.

Neither Lucy nor I were born here; Mendel came from Russia. In fact there is a feeling of the camp about Saskatoon, the temporary abode. At the university there are photographs of the town—in 1905 there were three frame buildings and a tent. In a bar I nearly came to blows with a man campaigning to preserve a movie theatre built in 1934. In Saskatoon that is ancient history, that is the cave painting at Lascaux. Lucy hails from an even newer settlement in the wild Peace River country where her father went to raise cattle and ended up a truck mechanic. Seven years ago she came to Saskatoon to work in a garment factory (her left hand bears a burn scar from a clothes press). Next fall she begins law school. Despite this evidence of intelligence, determination and ability, Lucy has no confidence in herself. In her mother's eyes she will never measure up and that is all that is important. I myself am a proud man and a gutter snob. I wear a ring in my left ear and my hair long. My parents migrated from a farm in Wisconsin to a farm in Saskatchewan in 1952 and still drive back every year to see the trees. I am two courses short of a degree in philosophy that I will never receive. I make my living at what comes to hand, house painting when I am wandering; since I settled with Lucy, I've worked as the lone overnight editor at the local newspaper. Against the bosses, I am a union man; against the union, I am an independent. When the publishers asked me to work days, I quit. That was a month ago. That was when Lucy knew I was leaving. Deep down she understands my nature. Mendel is another case: he was a butcher and a man who left traces. Now on the north bank of the river there are giant meat-packing plants spilling forth the odours of death, guts and excrement. Across the street are the holding pens for the cattle and the rail lines that bring them to slaughter. Before building his art gallery Mendel actually kept his paintings in this sprawling complex of buildings, inside the slaughter-house. If you went to his office, you sat in a waiting-room with a Picasso or a Roualt on the wall. Perhaps even a Van Gogh. The gallery is downriver at the opposite end of the city, very clean and modern. But whenever I go there I hear the panicky bellowing of the death-driven steers and see the streams of blood and the carcases and smell the stench and imagine the poor beasts rolling their eyes at Gauguin's green and luscious leaves as the bolt entered their brains.

We have decided to separate. It is a wintry Sunday after-noon. We are going to the Mendel Art Gallery. Watching Lucy shake her hair out and tuck it into her knitted hat, I suddenly feel close to tears. Behind her are the framed photographs of weathered prairie farmhouses, the vigorous spider plants, the scarred child's schooldesk where she does her studying, the brick-and-board bookshelf with her meagre library. (After eleven months there is still nothing of me that will remain.) This is an old song; there is no gesture of Lucy's that does not fill me instantly with pity, the child's hand held up to deflect the blow, her desperate attempts to conceal unworthiness. For her part she naturally sees me as the father who, in that earlier existence, proved so practised in evasion and flight. The fact that I am now leaving her only reinforces her intuition—it is as if she has expected it all along, almost as if she has been working toward it. This goes to show the force of initial impressions. For example, I will never forget the first time I saw Lucy. She was limping across Broadway, her feet swathed in bandages and jammed into her pumps, her face alternately distorted with agony and composed in dignity. I followed her for blocks—she was beautiful and wounded, the kind of woman I am always looking for to redeem me. Similarly, what she will always remember is that first night we spent together when all I did was hold her while she slept because, taking the bus home, she had seen a naked man masturbating in a window. Thus she had arrived at my door, laughing hysterically, afraid to stay at her own place alone, completely undone. At first she had played the temptress because she thought that was what I wanted. She kissed me hungrily and unfastened my shirt buttons. Then she ran into the bathroom and came out crying because she had dropped and broken the soap dish. That was when I put my arms around her and comforted her, which was what she had wanted from the beginning.

An apology for my style: I am not so much apologizing as invoking a tradition. Heraclitus, whose philosophy may not have been written in fragments but certainly comes to us in that form. Kierkegaard who mocked Hegel's system-building by writing everything as if it were an afterthought, *The Unscientific Postscript*. Nietzsche who wrote in aphorisms or what he called "attempts," dry runs at the subject matter, even arguing contradictory points of view in order to see all sides. Wittgenstein's *Investigations,* his fragmentary response to the architectonic of the earlier *Tractatus*. Traditional story writers compose a beginning, a middle and an end, string these together in a continuity as if there were some whole that they represented. Whereas I am writing fragments and discursive circumlocutions about an object that may not be complete or may be infinite. "Dog Attempts to Drown Man in Saskatoon" is my title, cribbed from a facetious newspaper headline. Lucy and I were married because of her feet and because she glimpsed a man masturbating in a window as her bus took her home from work. I feel that in discussing these occurences, these facts (our separation, the dog, the city, the weather, a trip to the art gallery) as constitutive of a non-system, I am peeling away some of the mystery of human life. I am also of the opinion that Mendel should have left the paintings in the slaughterhouse.

The discerning reader will by now have trapped me in a number of inconsistencies and doubtful statements. For example, we are not separating—I am leaving my wife and she has accepted that fact because it reaffirms her sense of herself as a person worthy of being left. Moreover it was wrong of me to pity her. Lucy is a quietly capable woman about to embark on what will inevitably be a successful career. She is not a waif nor could she ever redeem me with her suffering. Likewise she was wrong to view me as forever gentle and forbearing in the sexual department. And finally I suspect that there was more than coincidence in the fact that she spotted the man in his window on my night off from the newspaper. I do not doubt that she saw the man; he is a recurring nightmare of Lucy's. But whether she saw him that particular night, or some night in the past, or whether she made him up out of whole cloth and came to believe in him, I cannot say. About her feet, however, I have been truthful. That day she had just come from her doctor after having the stitches removed.

Lucy's clumsiness. Her clumsiness stems from the fact that she was born with six toes on each foot. This defect, I'm sure, had something to do with the way her mother mistreated her. Among uneducated folk there is often a feeling that physical anomalies reflect mental flaws. And as a kind of punishment for being born (and afterwards because her brother had died), Lucy's feet were never looked at by a competent doctor. It wasn't until she was 26 and beginning to enjoy a new life that she underwent a painful operation to have the vestigial digits excised. This surgery left her big toes all but powerless; now they flop like stubby, white worms at the ends of her feet. Where she had been a schoolgirl athlete with six toes, she became awkward and ungainly with five.

Her mother, Celeste, is one of those women who make feminism a *cause célèbre*—no, that is being glib. Truthfully, she was never any man's slave. I have the impression that after the first realization, the first inkling that she had married the wrong man, she entered into the role of submissive female with a strange, destructive gusto. She seems to have had an immoderate amount of hate in her, enough to spread its poison among many people who touched her in a kind of negative of the parable of loaves and fishes. And the man, the father, was not so far as I can tell cruel, merely ineffectual, just the wrong man. Once, years later, Lucy and Celeste were riding on a bus together when Celeste pointed to a man sitting a few seats ahead and said, "That is the man I loved." That was all she ever said on the topic and the man himself was a balding, petty, functionary type, completely uninteresting except in terms of the exaggerated passion Celeste had invested in him over the years. Soon after Lucy's father married Celeste he realized he would never be able to live with her—he absconded for the army, abandoning her with the first child in a drover's shack on a cattle baron's estate. (From time to time Lucy attempts to write about her childhood—her stories always seem unbelievable—a world of infanticide, blood feuds and brutality. I can barely credit these tales seeing her so prim and composed, not prim but you know how she sits very straight in her chair and her hair is always in place and her clothes are expensive if not quite stylish and her manners are correct without being at all natural; Lucy is composed in the sense of being made up or put together out of pieces, not in the sense of being tranquil. But nevertheless she carries these *cauchemars* in her head: the dead babies found beneath the fencerow, blood on sheets, shotgun blasts in the night, her brother going under the highway roller, her mother's cruel silence.) The father fled as I say. He sent them money-orders, three-quarters of his pay, to that point he was responsible. Celeste never spoke of him and his infrequent visits home were always a surprise to the children; his visits and the locked bedroom door and the hot, breathy silence of what went on behind the door; Celeste's rising vexation and hysteria; the new pregnancy; the postmarks on the money-orders. Then the boy died. Perhaps he was Celeste's favourite, a perfect one to hold over the tall, already beautiful, monster with six toes and (I conjecture again) her father's look. The boy died and the house went silent—Celeste had forbidden a word to be spoken—and this was the worst for Lucy, the cold parlour circumspection of Protestant mourning. They did not utter a redeeming sound, only replayed the image of the boy running, laughing, racing the machine, then tripping and going under, being sucked under—Lucy did not even see the body, and in an access of delayed grief almost two decades later she would tell me she had always assumed he just flattened out like a cartoon character. Celeste refused to weep; only her hatred grew like a heavy weight against her children. And in that vacuum, that terrible silence accorded all feeling and especially the mysteries of sex and death, the locked door of the bedroom and the shut coffin lid, the absent father and the absent brother, somehow became inextricably entwined in Lucy's mind; she was only ten, a most beautiful monster, surrounded by absent gods and a bitter worship. So that when she saw the naked man calmly masturbating in the upper storey window from her bus, framed as it were under the cornice of a Saskatoon rooming-house, it was for her like a vision of the centre of the mystery, the scene behind the locked door, the corpse in its coffin, God, and she immediately imagined her mother waiting irritably in the shadow just out of sight with a towel to wipe the sperm from the windowpane, aroused, yet almost fainting at the grotesque denial of her female passion.

Do not, if you wish, believe any of the above. It is psychological jazz written *en marge*; I am a poet of marginalia. Some of what I write is utter crap and wishful thinking. Lucy is not "happy to be sad"; she is seething inside because I am betraying her. Her anger gives her the courage to make jokes; she blushes when I laugh because she still hopes that I will stay. Of course, my willingness to accompany her to the art gallery is inspired by guilt. She is completely aware of this fact. Her invitation is premeditated, manipulative. No gesture is lost; all our acts are linked and repeated. She is, after all, Celeste's daughter. Also, do not believe for a moment that I hate that woman for what she was. That instant on the bus in a distant town when she pointed out the man she truly loved she somehow redeemed herself for Lucy and for me, showing herself receptive of forgiveness and pity. Nor do I hate Lucy though I am leaving her.

My wife and I decide to separate, and then suddenly we are almost happy together. I repeat this crucial opening sentence for the purpose of reminding myself of my general intention. In a separate notebook next to me (vodka on ice sweating onto and blurring the ruled pages) I have a list of subjects to cover: 1) blindness (the man the dog led into the river was blind); 2) a man I know who was gored by a bison (real name to be withheld); 3) Susan the weaver and her little girl and the plan for us to live in Pelican Narrows; 4) the wolves at the city zoo; 5) the battlefields of Batoche and Duck Lake; 6) bridge symbolism; 7) a fuller description of the death of Lucy's brother; 8) three photographs of Lucy in my possession; 9) my wish to have met Mendel (he is dead) and be his friend; 10) the story of the story, or how the dog tried to drown the man in Saskatoon.

Call this a play. Call me Orestes. Call her mother Clytemnestra. Her father, the wandering warrior king. (When he died accidentally a year ago, they sent Lucy his diary. Every day of his life he had recorded the weather; that was all.) Like everyone else, we married because we thought we could change one another. I was the brother-friend come to slay the tyrant Celeste; Lucy was to teach me the meaning of suffering. But there is no meaning and in the labyrinth of Lucy's mind the spirit of her past eluded me. Take sex for instance. She is taller than I am; people sometimes think she must be a model. She is without a doubt the most beautiful woman I have been to bed with. Yet there is no passion, no arousal. Between the legs she is as dry as a prairie summer. I am tender, but tenderness is no substitute for biology. Penetration is always painful. She gasps, winces. She will not perform oral sex though sometimes she likes having it done to her, providing she can overcome her embarrassment. What she does love is for me to wrestle her to the living-room carpet and strip her clothes off in a mock rape. She squeals and protests and then scampers naked to the bedroom where she waits impatiently while I get undressed. Only once have I detected her orgasm—this while she sat on my lap fully clothed and I manipulated her with my fingers. It goes without saying she will not talk about these things. She protects herself from herself and there is never any feeling that we are together. When Lucy's periods began, Celeste told her she had cancer. More than

167

once she was forced to eat garbage from a dog's dish. Sometimes her mother would simply lock her out of the house for the night. These stories are shocking; Celeste was undoubtedly mad. By hatred, mother and daughter are manacled together for eternity. "You can change," I say with all my heart. "A woman who only sees herself as a victim never gets wise to herself." "No," she says, touching my hand sadly. "Ah! Ah!" I think, between weeping and words. Nostalgia is form; hope is content. Lucy is an empty building, a frenzy of restlessness, a soul without a future. And I fling out in desperation, Orestes-like, seeking my own Athens and release.

More bunk! I'll let you know now that we are not going to the art gallery as I write this. Everything happened some time ago and I am living far away in another country. (Structuralists would characterize my style as "robbing the signifier of the signified." My opening sentence, my premise, is now practically destitute of meaning, or it means everything. Really, this is what happens when you try to tell the truth about something; you end up like the snake biting its own tail. There are a hundred reasons why I left Lucy. I don't want to seem shallow. I don't want to say, well, I was a meat-and-potatoes person and she was a vegetarian, or that I sometimes believe she simply orchestrated the whole fiasco, seduced me, married me and then refused to be a wife—yes, I would prefer to think that I was guiltless, that I didn't just wander off fecklessly like her father. To explain this, or for that matter to explain why the dog led the man into the river, you have to explain the world, even God—if we accept Godel's theorem regarding the unjustifiability of systems from within. Everything is a symbol of everything else. Or everything is a symbol of death as Levi-Strauss says. In other words, there is no signified and life is nothing but a long haunting. Perhaps that is all that I am trying to say....) However, we *did* visit the art gallery one winter Sunday near the end of our eleven-month marriage. There were two temporary exhibitions and all of Mendel's slaughterhouse pictures had been stored in the basement. One wing was devoted to photographs of grain elevators, very phallic with their little overhanging roofs. We laughed about this together; Lucy was kittenish, pretending to be shocked. Then she walked across the hall alone to contemplate the acrylic prairie-scapes by local artists. I descended the stairs to drink coffee and watch the frozen river. This was downstream from the Idylwyld Bridge where the fellow went in (there is an open stretch of two or three hundred yards where a hot-water outlet prevents the river from freezing over completely) and it occurred to me that if he had actually drowned, if the current had dragged him under the ice, they wouldn't have found his body until the spring breakup. And probably they would have discovered it hung up on the weir, which I could see from the gallery window.

Forget it. A bad picture: Lucy upstairs "appreciating" art, me downstairs thinking of bodies under the ice. Any moment now she will come skipping toward me flushed with excitement after a successful cultural adventure. That is not what I meant to show you. That Lucy is not a person, she is a caricature. When legends are born, people die. Rather, let us look at the place where all reasons converge. No. Let me tell you how Lucy is redeemed: preamble and anecdote. Her greatest fear is that she will turn into Celeste. Naturally, she is becoming more and more like her mother every day without noticing it. She has the financial independence Celeste no doubt craved, and she has been disappointed in love. Three times. The first man made himself into a wandering rage with drugs. The second was an adulterer. Now me. Already she is acquiring an edge of bitterness, of why-me-ness. But, and this is an Everest of a but, the woman can dance! I don't mean at the disco or in a ballroom; I don't mean she studied ballet. We were strolling in Diefenbaker Park one summer day shortly after our wedding (this is on the bluffs overlooking Mendel's meatpacking plant) when we came upon a puppet show. It was some sort of children's fair: there were petting zoos, pony rides, candy stands, bicycles being given away as prizes, all that kind of thing in addition to the puppets. It was a famous troupe that had started in the sixties as part of the counter-culture movement—I need not mention the name. The climax of the performance was a stately dance by two giant puppets perhaps 30 feet tall, a man and a woman, backwoods types. We arrived just in time to see the woman rise from the ground, supported by three puppeteers. She rises from the grass stiffly then spreads her massive arms toward the man and an orchestra begins a reel. It is an astounding sight. I notice that the children in the audience are rapt. And suddenly I am aware of Lucy, her face aflame, this crazy grin and her eyes dazzled. She is looking straight up at the giant woman. The music, as I say, begins and the puppet sways and opens her arms towards her partner (they are both very stern, very grave) and Lucy begins to sway and spread her arms. She lifts her feet gently, one ofter the other, begins to turn, then swings back. She doesn't know what she is doing; this is completely unself-conscious. There is only Lucy and the puppets and the dance. She is a child again and I am in awe of her innocence. It is a scene that brings a lump to my throat: the high, hot, summer sun, the children's faces like flowers in a sea of grass, the towering, swaying puppets, and Lucy lost in herself. Lucy, dancing. Probably she no longer remembers this incident. At the time, or shortly after, she said, "Oh no! Did I really? Tell me I didn't do that!" She was laughing, not really embarrassed. "Did anyone see me?" And when the puppeteers passed the hat at the end of their show, I turned out my pockets, I gave them everything I had.

I smoke Gitanes. I like to drink in an Indian bar on 20th Street near Eaton's. My nose was broken in a car accident when I was eighteen; it grew back crooked. I speak softly; sometimes I stutter. I don't like crowds. In my spare time, I paint large pictures of the city. Photographic realism is my style. I work on a pencil grid using egg tempera because it's better for detail. I do shopping-centres, old movie theatres that are about to be torn down, slaughterhouses. While everyone else is looking out at the prairie, I peer inward and record what is merely transitory, what is human. Artifice. Nature defeats me. I cannot paint ripples on a lake, or the movement of leaves, or a woman's face. Like most people, I suppose, my heart is broken because I cannot be what I wish to be. On the day in question, one of the coldest of the year, I hike down from the university along Saskatchewan Drive over-looking the old railway hotel, the modest office blocks, the ice-shrouded gardens of the city. I carry a camera, snapping end-of-the-world photos for a future canvas. At the Third Avenue Bridge I pause to admire the lattice of I-beams, black against the frozen mist swirling up from the river and the translucent exhaust plumes of the ghostly cars shuttling to and fro. Crossing the street, I descend the wooden steps into Rotary Park, taking two more shots of the bridge at a close angle before the film breaks from the cold. I swing round, focusing on the squat ugliness of the Idylwyld Bridge with its fat concrete piers obscuring the view upriver, and then suddenly an icy finger seems to touch my heart: out on the river, on the very edge of the snowy crust where the turbid waters from the outlet pipe churn and steam, a black dog is playing. I refocus. The dog scampers in a tight circle, races toward the brink, skids to a stop, barks furiously at something in the grey water. I stumble forward a step or two. Then I see the man, swept downstream, bobbing in the current, his arms flailing stiffly. In another instant, the dog leaps after him, disappears, almost as if I had dreamed it. I don't quite know what I am doing, you understand. The river is no-man's-land. First I am plunging through the knee-deep snow of the park. Then I lose my footing on the bank and find myself sliding on my seat onto the river ice. Before I have time to think, "There is a man in the river," I am sprinting to intercept him, struggling to untangle the camera from around my neck, stripping off my coat. I have forgotten momentarily how long it takes exposed skin to freeze and am lost in a frenzy of speculation upon the impossibility of existence in the river, the horror of the current dragging you under the ice at the end of the open water, the creeping numbness, again the impossibility, the alienness of the idea itself, the dog and the man immersed. I feel the ice rolling under me, throw myself flat, wrapped in a gentle terror, then inch forward again, spread-eagled, throwing my coat by a sleeve, screaming, "Catch it! Catch it!" to the man whirling toward me, scrabbling with bloody hands at the crumbling ledge. All this occupies less time than it takes to tell. He is a strange bearlike creature, huge in an old duffel coat with its hood up, steam rising around him, his face bloated and purple, his red hands clawing at the ice shelf, an inhuman "awing" sound emanating from his throat, his eyes rolling upwards. He makes no effort to reach the coat sleeve trailed before him as the current carries him by. Then the dog appears, paddling toward the man, straining to keep its head above the choppy surface.

The dog barks, rests a paw on the man's shoulder, seems to drag him under a little, and then the man is striking out wildly, fighting the dog off, being twisted out into the open water by the eddies. I see the leather hand harness flapping from the dog's neck and suddenly the full horror of the situation assails me: the man is blind. Perhaps he understands nothing of what is happening to him, the world gone mad, this freezing hell. At the same moment, I feel strong hands grip my ankles and hear another's laboured breathing. I look over my shoulder. There is a pink-cheeked policeman with a thin yellow moustache stretched on the ice behind me. Behind him, two teenage boys are in the act of dropping to all fours, making a chain of bodies. A fifth person, a young woman, is running toward us. "He's blind," I shout. The policeman nods: he seems to comprehend everything in an instant. The man in the water has come to rest against a jutting point of ice a few yards away. The dog is much nearer, but I make for the man, crawling on my hands and knees, forgetting my coat. There seems nothing to fear now. Our little chain of life reaching toward the blind drowning man seems sufficient against the infinity of forces that have culminated in this moment. The crust is rolling and bucking beneath us as I take his wrists. His fingers, hard as talons, lock into mine. Immediately he ceases to utter that terrible, unearthly bawling sound. Inching backward, I somehow contrive to lever the dead weight of his body over the ice lip, then drag him on his belly like a sack away from the water. The cop turns him gently on his back; he is breathing in gasps, his eyes rolling frantically. "Tank you. Tank you," he whispers, his strength gone. The others quickly remove their coats and tuck them around the man who now looks like some strange beached fish, puffing and muttering in the snow. Then in the eerie silence that follows, broken only by the shushing sound of traffic on the bridges, the distant whine of a siren coming nearer, the hissing river and my heart beating, I look into the smoky water once more and see that the dog is gone. I am dazed; I watch a drop of sweat freezing on the policeman's moustache. I stare into the grey flux where it slips quietly under the ice and disappears. One of the boys offers me a cigarette. The blind man moans; he says, "I go home now. Dog good. I all right. I walk home." The boys glance at each other. The woman is shivering. Everything seems empty and anticlimactic. We are shrouded in enigma. The policeman takes out a notebook, a tiny symbol of rationality, scribbled words against the void. As an ambulance crew skates a stretcher down the river bank, he begins to ask the usual questions, the usual, unanswerable questions.

This is not the story I wanted to tell. I repeat this *caveat* as a reminder that I am wilful and wayward as a storyteller, not a good storyteller at all. The right story, the true story, had I been able to tell it, would have changed your life—but it is buried, gone, lost. The next day Lucy and I drive to the spot where I first saw the dog. The river is once more sanely empty and the water boils quietly where it has not yet frozen. Once more I tell her how it happened, but she prefers the public version, what she hears on the radio or reads in the newspaper, to my disjointed impressions. It is also true that she knows she is losing me and she is at the stage where it is necessary to deny strenuously all my values and perceptions. She wants to think that I am just like her father or that I always intended to humiliate her. The facts of the case are that the man and dog apparently set out to cross the Idylwyld Bridge but turned off along the approach and walked into the water, the man a little ahead of the dog. In the news account, the dog is accused of insanity, dereliction of duty and a strangely uncanine malevolence. "Dog Attempts to Drown Man," the headline reads. Libel law prevents speculation on the human victim's mental state, his intentions. The dog is dead, but the tone is jocular. *Dog Attempts to Drown Man.* All of which means that no-one knows what happened from the time he fell into the river and we are free to invent structures and symbols as we see fit. The man survives, it seems, his strange baptism, his trial by cold and water. I know in my own mind that he appeared exhausted, not merely from the experience of near-drowning, but from before, in spirit, while the dog seemed eager and alert. We know, or at least we can all agree to theorize, that a bridge is a symbol of change (one side to the other, hence death), of connection (the marriage of opposites), but also of separation from the river of life, a bridge is an object of culture. Perhaps man and dog chose together to walk through the pathless snows to the water's edge and throw themselves into uncertainty. The man was blind as are we all; perhaps he sought illumination in the frothing waste. Perhaps they went as old friends. Or perhaps the dog accompanied the man only reluctantly, the man forcing the dog to lead him across the ice. I saw the dog swim to him, saw the man fending the dog off. Perhaps the dog was trying to save its master, or perhaps it was only playing, not understanding in the least what was happening. Whatever is the case my allegiance is with the dog; the man is too human, too predictable. But man and dog together are emblematic—that is my impression at any rate—they are the mind and spirit, the one blind, the other dumb; one defeated, the other naive and hopeful, both forever going out. And I submit that after all the simplified explanations and crude jokes about the blind man and his dog, the act is full of a strange and terrible mystery, of beauty.

My wife and I decide to separate, and then suddenly we are almost happy together. But this was long ago, as was the visit to the Mendel Art Gallery and my time in Saskatoon. And though the moment when Lucy is shaking down her hair and tucking it into her knitted cap goes on endlessly in my head as does the reverberation of that other moment when the dog disappears under the ice, there is much that I have already forgotten. I left Lucy because she was too real, too hungry for love, while I am a dreamer. There are two kinds of courage: the courage that holds things together and the courage that throws them away. The first is more common; it is the cement of civilization; it is Lucy's. The second is the courage of drunks and suicides and mystics. My sign is impurity. By leaving, you understand, I proved that I was unworthy. I have tried to write Lucy since that winter—her only response has been to return my letters unopened. This is appropriate. She means for me to read them myself, those tired, clotted apologies. I am the writer of the words; she knows well enough they are not meant for her. But my words are sad companions and sometimes I remember... well...the icy water is up to my neck and I hear the ghost dog barking, she tried to warn me; yes, yes, I say, but I was blind.

Under the Hill

Marian Engel

I was tired that evening, tired to the point of being moth-eaten and frail. Ben caught me dozing in the living-room. "You've been out there again," he said. "Why do you do it?"

"One, I'm a nationalist, two, I'm a Terryberry-watcher, three, I'm the Cancer Society Lady, four, I'm meals-on-wheels, five, she's my friend."

"Would you fall over if you had a drink with me?"

"Check the oven when you're in the kitchen, will you?"

When the children were halfway through high school I

wanted to go back into the workforce with the rest of my generation, but Ben was against. it. "Not on principle," he said, "but because I'm a selfish bastard." I would have fought him on the principle, but the selfishness got to me. Ben and I have a lot in common, that way. And there aren't many jobs in Indigo. And I hated teaching when I was single.

So I busied myself in the way of middle-aged women, doing good works and visiting the sick, collecting material for county Archives: living the life of Ladies in Hats, a life for which I had had contempt when I was young. We didn't need a second income, but I needed more contact with other minds, other sets of feelings and experiences. I don't know how my mother and her friends endured their captivity. The drink Ben poured me was a stiff one. "You always sound jealous of Iris," I said. The weak spring sun slanted through the window-panes and lit up the last of the forced hyacinths on the coffee-table. They suddenly exhaled a waft of perfume and the place smelled like a funeral parlour.

"You come home tired from her."

"Do you know what we did today?"

"You look as if you turned out the attic."

"We sat in the forecourt and went through the button box. She had a bunch of those weights they used to put in women's skirts to keep them from blowing around. I'd forgotten." I like Ben because he's genuinely gregarious, he likes people and is interested in everything about them.

"And then you cleaned the kitchen sink, emptied the chamber-pot, scalded the pots and pans and made tea."

"Well, that. And when I emptied the chamber, she piped up, 'A centipede a pint and a millipede a quart'; my bit of folklore for the day. I must put it in the notebook." I got up and kissed him on his rising forehead. "I'd have sat in the sun with you, Ben, if you were there to sit with." In the voice I used to use for Little Ben.

Ben doesn't sit in the sun; he likes running around and doing all those things you do in the good rich middle part of your life when you know a lot and still have energy, like making fast deals and playing fast squash. He's not ready to sit back and admire life yet. I passed into that category when I was ill last year.

Perhaps, however, it is not so much ageing and weakness that makes me able to sit quietly with her, walled away from the elements in the little square between house, greenhouse and drive shed, in the ell between the blue potting-sheds and the lilyfield, shaded by elm and esker. I was a dreamy, quiet child and I love my life when it's sluggish as a fat green river. Mrs. Boronski does the cleaning, Palmer's delivers the groceries, Ben makes his own breakfast; I have time for Iris.

And I've been a Terryberry-watcher for a long time. My mother was one before, and the whole community has been from time to time. They've never been quite like other people. They've always been first off to wars and goldrushes, taking up land in the west or California lifestyles long before the rest of us. They're bellwethers, or opportunists, depending on how you think. The first divorced man in Indigo was Dennis Terryberry, the dentist, Tossie was our first OBE, for nursing in World War I, the judge was always a man to watch in his white summer suit, ribboned *pince-nez* and a rosebud in his lapel as if it were the Legion of Honour. Dr. Carscadden is thinking of declaring Ronnie our first case of confirmed Alzheimer's disease—though he appears to have had it most of his life—and then there's Iris.

I didn't grow up in Indigo, but Mother was from here and I knew the town from visits to innumerable farm relatives on the periphery and trips in (in the buggy during

the war: how we loved them!) to the Co-op and the cream-
ery. When Ben and I moved here the first Terryberry I
met was Mrs. Wilt Terryberry, the undertaker's wife, an
abrasive woman if ever there was one. I remember asking
her for a division of a particularly lovely peony she had.
"Buy your own," she snarled. I was so hurt I didn't mention it to anyone for months. Then I told Mary Gaskin,
who said, "Oh, but she wanted you to go to Iris." When I
said, "Who's Iris?", another part of my life began.

*Terryberry's Favourite: rich mauve standards, flamboyant violet
falls heavily ruffled and gartered in purple. Try a cluster of
chorus girls at your door. Mid-season, $4 and worth it.*

I went to university because Mother had wanted to go.
She was like that, felt I should live the life she had failed
to have. She said I shouldn't cry because Bill Fairchild
married someone else, careers were the thing for women
now, teaching, that would sustain me. It wasn't pearls
before swine for me, it was decaying mangels to scrawny
chicken. Then Mother summoned me back to London
because she was ill, and for something to get me out of
the house I took up giving English lessons to newly
arrived immigrants. Ben was new to the country but
never young. He was fascinated by the beauty and avail-
ability of old brick farmhouses in the area, talked me into
buying the old Elder place. Mother thought it a poor
investment and as for my marrying a poor "Bohemian"
immigrant (we used a word she might like if not understand) who sold insurance to farmers—Ben thought she
was funny and tugged me away from her to a life of rescu-
ing old houses and raising children.

And since houses and children go with flowers, I
started to make gardens, filling them with peonies with
the lushness of nursing mothers, scarlet military poppies,

starry-eyed phlox and trusses of daylilies and iris, which I eventually started to buy from Miss Terryberry, "The one who never married."

At first I couldn't find the place, expecting sun glinting on greenhouses in a wide field. Iris' establishment was screened from the road by a clump of cedar, and built into the side of the northfacing ridge of gravel that gives this countryside its character, the Long Esker. Her house was a vague arrangement of shanties and chimney pots she had brought from another site and attached to one wing of the glass houses in order to save on heat. The arrangement looked scatty and rundown the day I first went there, looking among stacks of bagged fertilizer, stray kittens and brown dogs for a sign that said "Office" and finding none. "We aren't what we were," she said when I found her, "but maybe I have something you want."

Judge's Fancy: full-headed, showy magenta, double peony that visibly struts in the field. Mid-season, long-lasting. Isolate this colour from the others and its appeal will double.

It makes me boil with anger when people say Canadians have no history. When I was a child I wondered if I would ever escape from the tales of ingrown passion and petty quarrels the matrix of Scots-Irish and English in the county bred. One got tired of waggons breaking down at the right fence corner, horses pausing before sleeping babies in fields, wrong-headed marriages and elopements to Chicago, diptheria deaths (always the pretty daughter: the plain one pulled through), losses to foreign wars. I was one of the generation that tried for a while to cover that porous historical brick and wood with the hard tile of sophistication, dropping the last of the forced handicrafts, feeding on the new and glittering values imported from postwar Europe; but I too returned to the matrix and raised children and found I needed after all grey churches, things hanging from rafters, bleeding-heart.

Terry's Favourite: rich mauve standards, violet falls, heavily ruffled, veined purple, rosy stamens, tall, a sensation, $5.95 and worth every penny.

She didn't talk much at first, but there were things I wanted that opened her up to me: monkshood, cottage pinks. She was famous far beyond the boundaries of the county for her old flowers, iris, daylily, peonies, single roses.

"The judge got us all around the dining-room table when I was maybe eight or nine and read us the riot act about making something for ourselves, even the girls," she said. "There was nothing worse than greed without ambition, he said, and there was a lot of it in this house —Mother was a wonderful cook and there seemed to be barrels of sugar cookies in the kitchen—and in general he fired us up. George went into law, Dennis figured the county needed a dentist, and he'd have done all right if he hadn't taken up with poor Lily Mills, no brains and no health, though she was a pretty, pale thing—and Tossie went for nursing. He wanted me to train for a teacher but I didn't like the idea any more than you liked the fact, and I always liked the garden. He'd have let me stay home if I was any good around the house, but I was clumsy and dreamy, so he got me work as a trainee with a breeder he knew in Holland, Michigan. Mother might have objected to my going away so soon: I was only sixteen—but she was completely taken up with Ronnie by then, and Wilt was off somewhere learning to be an undertaker.

"He was a fair man, the judge, and well-liked, though I didn't like him. Whatever you said, he had to go one better. When I was about fifteen, I remember your mother's brother Will came calling on a Sunday after-noon, and I liked him; but we were playing some kind of parlour game and he said he wasn't going in with any cut-throat Terryberrys, and that was that.

"Father fought me all the way. When he saw me work-ing in greenhouses, he decided it wasn't a good job for a lady. This piece of land was known as Uncle Beau's Bog before I bought it with my savings. I camped out here in a tent the first summer. Father fussed and fumed and I let him. First he bought me a dog, then he helped me set up a cottage: just a bare shelter, one of the drivesheds from behind Wilt's. He said the whole enterprise was bad for his reputation. I didn't care. I'd never had a come-hither eye. There's no glamour in men to a girl with four broth-ers.

"I didn't give a darn about my personal life. I put everything I had into getting the business going. I wanted to show him I could do something. In the twen-ties this was a good go-ahead business, and in the thirties it was famous, though the problem was always the same: when times were good, you couldn't get help, and when there was help, nobody had any money for flowers. I spe-cialized in spring perennials because if you've got the patience for them, the return is good. Of course then we sold a lot of shrubs and bushfruit and the usual box plants: styles change but petunias and marigolds are the things that do well.

"He was an old tyrant. Father. When he was dying I went into Indigo every night to sit with him. He'd worry away at me, 'Iris, Iris, you never married.' I used to think, 'Men are weak creatures, they have to be placated with pie. I'd get elected prime minister, he'd never notice.' That was the year I took medals at four exhibi-tions here and two in Michigan. I was just an old maid to him."

Terry's Treasure: 28" daylily, early, a miracle: velvet petals a heavily ruffled apricot; green throat circled pale gold. Rich, meaty clusters, well-branched and graceful. Colour holds all day, a prize-winner.

"Now here are the old catalogues. We couldn't afford colour printing, but Wilt's daughter Jessie did me a few little drawings like that phlox. Mr. Jackson set it up every year for me in the fall, when I knew what was going to be ready for spring. I started out very scientific, but I discovered that what people want isn't science, it's novelty, a blue version of a yellow flower or a bigger one, or a night flower that stays open all day: something their neighbourhood doesn't have already.

"Still, you don't want to go too far with fashion. The nights are long out here, and the flowers don't talk much, so I used to read a lot, philosophy, even, and I remember somebody saying something about all the things tending to something—well, in the nursery world, I'll tell you, all things tend to puce. When you see in a catalogue some kind of brown sliding into purple with a green sort of sheen, you know some beggar's made a mistake and he's trying to pass it off. You keep your yellows and your purples segregated and get back to Eden where colours ran true."

Ben's insecurities start leaking out when I pay too much attention to anyone else, so I didn't see as much as I wanted to of Iris, but after she broke her hip, when I was with her and counted the number of painful motions she went through even to boil an egg for herself, I started taking her out the meals-on-wheels for dinner, and little lunches of the kind the children and I always loved: a slice of Granny Smith apple cut like a wheel, a crunch of cheddar cheese, a few wheat crackers and a spoonful of cherry jam with a thermos of good coffee. We'd sit in the sunlight like children in a nursery and eat, and then I'd check on her exercises. The doctor was dubious about the hip operation, thought that at her age she might as well take to her bed, but Wilt's nephew Brian Stewart is resident in orthopaedics at one of the big hospitals in London and he got his boss, who is world famous, to insert a prosthesis. They had her up the next day and hobbling on canes in a week, but efficient movement was still a long way off, that day.

"Dr. Carscadden's a fine man," she said, "but I don't think he's fond of me. A lot of people aren't. They think I'm a crazy old witch, they think there was something between Ardeen and me, they think I should go into a home with Ronnie.

"Ronnie was always the funny one. Mother took a look at him the minute he was born and said, 'That one's mine, I'll keep him,' and let him stay a child forever. Ever notice women with big families doing that, keeping the smallest boy for a priest, the one who won't be unfaithful to her?

"Father wasn't much help. He'd be away three months on the circuit and come back grumpy and formal. The tone of the house would change completely. He scared the living daylights out of us: he'd yell at Mother, 'What, no applesauce for tea, what do you mean, woman?' and she'd throw her apron over her face and cry. Tossie said it was a game, but Ronnie and I thought he scared her as much as he scared us. At least I got out in time. Still, he's all right in the Home, Ronnie, he's been senile all his life, his first and second childhoods all mixed up.

"Carscadden was hard on me about Ardeen. He thought I overworked her, but she was one of those terriers, worked all night and all day as if the devil were after her. I didn't know she had a bad heart. She'd had a hard upbringing, all that stuff about the devil finding work for

185

idle hands to do. You know what that's about. What I say is, if the good lord meant us not to play with ourself, what was he doing making our arms just the right length?

"I loved Ardeen, I guess, but not in a physical way. There must have been something missing in me, the sex-urge didn't come out, or maybe I didn't let myself feel it. Oh, there was a man in Michigan when I was young: a tall, fair, quiet chap with a limp—ever notice how young girls are wild for a man with a limp?—and we'd stand there playing with anthers and stamens and pistils and kind of lean toward each other, but he never said anything, and when you work twelve hours a day, you don't have much energy."

Ardeen: a clear blue beauty, silver shimmers in the graceful falls, silver-spangled beard. Perfect form, good substance, the grand duchess of irises, where else can you purchase charm and dignity?

"She just walked in off the road one day and stood by my elbow and after about half an hour said, 'Can I have a job Miss Terryberry?' I was hard up then, I'd have taken a one-legged leper, there was work for twenty. I needed a bunch of POWs like the ones I had in the war, instead I was making do with a couple of hired hands. Carscadden says I worked her to death, but she was one of those driven people, and she'd been raped by the field hands working for a man outside Leamington, she was trying to get it out of her mind. She asked where the bunkhouse was but I put her in the spare room.

"There was all that fuss when Freud said everything was sex; in this part of the world people certainly think it is. They don't want to admit their own feelings so they accuse everyone else of it. They used to say right out Ardeen and I were a pair of lezzies. She was a poor sad thing, and I'd hear her sobbing in the night and go in and make her drink strawberry tea and a couple of times I put my arms around her to comfort her, but I wanted company, not sex, and she never offered me any. She followed me like a shadow, and I'm human; I lapped up her dumb devotion.

"Those were good years. It isn't complicated work. You have to be orderly and keep good records, marking what you crossed with A or B, and what you bred on itself and what you let the bees do. The big perennials take a long time to make a show, but you can propagate the roots and get them to run true. The return isn't great in this country, we don't have American megalomania or British estates, but there's a small steady market for good stock. The climate doesn't let us go any further: when there's only five months of decent weather, naturally you think cucumbers instead of rhododendrons. We did all right, and I wasn't a man with a wife to keep in diamonds and furs. Ardeen never asked for anything. When she got shabby I'd take her up to London and dress her as if she were my child.

"She couldn't talk in front of strangers except to say yes, no, it likes a bit of lime, but she was bright around the house in the evening when we had time to talk. She helped me clean out the library. She liked science fiction. She worked on primroses for a while, she called them her space flowers, but they don't do well here. She fancied Japaneses things, too, and she did a bit of Japanese gardening, training chrysanthemums to fancy patterns and making bonsai trees, but she did better under orders than working on her own. She might have got better if she'd lived.

"The mistake I made was thinking she was thin because she was like me, one of the earth'd stringy beasts. She's get awful coughs and I'd doctor her with garlic soup, whatever was lying around. Neither of us ate much. Then one winter I made her go to Jack Carscadden and it was lungs. He was so mad at me! Cooping her up in a greenhouse he said was the last thing I should have done with her.

"I was afraid they'd take her away from me and put her in the San, but they don't do that any more. The antibiotics fixed her up, but by that time she was weak in the heart. I got this sort of courtyard arrangement fixed up so she could sit in the sun when there was any, but she died that winter. She wouldn't tell anyone who her parents were, so I was registered as her next of kin. She never got any mail when she was here, not so much as a postcard, and there are a lot of Bakers in the world, though not many Ardeens. I felt she might be a Maritimer from her accent, but nobody answered my ad in the Halifax paper. There aren't many people who come and go like the wind, but a few do."

Major General: narrow, erect royal-blue standards, lighter blue falls netted and veined royal; button-brass beard. Stiff, dignified, gleams in the sun, good against roses.

I was tired when I got home that night, and the next day Nancy Fairbanks went out to see Iris, so I stayed home to prepare for the Historical Society meeting. We had a turnout of 45 to hear a woman from Toronto recite verses and songs from Alice Kane's book about her Ulster childhood and it was well after midnight, and raining, by the time they were able to leave off their reminiscences—one song inevitably produced another and to judge from the way we all knew them, we were all from Bally-some-where—and go home. I woke tired the next day and Ben said he hadn't much to do, why didn't I stay in bed that day, he would call on Iris, and to tell the truth I was grateful.

Rest did its magic, however, and by five I had a good dinner on and was expecting him from the window. There was no sign of him until much later and I was reading in the study when the car drove in. He came in the side door without calling out, and I heard him rummaging for ice and glasses at once, a bad sign. Then the kitchen drawers opening and shutting; he was looking for something. He came toward me limping, mud on his trousers, a scowl on his face. "For God's sake where's the garlic, I've found the string not the garlic."

"Under the onions."

He handed me the drinks and went back, returned knotting a necklace of string and garlic around his neck. "Whatever happened, Ben?"

"Well, I went out and found her. She's all right. Mud in your eye!"

"Mud on you."

"Serves me right for a visiting bastard. She's a witch."

"Sit down and tell me about it."

"Okay, Mummy." But first he got himself a second drink. "Well, I got out there about three, and first I got stuck in the lane. Then when I went to the door there wasn't any answer, and just as I was going to the side to see if I could get through a window in case she was dead on the floor, there was a scurrying and this— creature—came to the door; it had short red hair in a brush cut and a long dress striped like a bumblebee. Have you heard of someone called Cordell Wainwright?"

"Oh, Ben, you and Della in the same house!" It made me giggle.

"Well, we were, and it was something, I don't care how famous the guy is, he's weird."

"You didn't come to Canada to turn into a redneck. What was he up to?"

"He had a big portfolio of flower drawings he was doing for her and then he did a sort of dance for me, at her insistence, about being a bumblebee. I think they were laughing at me."

"Probably. Iris gets silly when she's with him. He's a wonderful designer, though."

"You couldn't say the drawings were bad, they were a world, they drew me in, they scared the hell out of me. I mean at first they just looked like flowers and then I realized they were, well—perverse."

"He has a way of making things look fleshy and over-blown."

"She gave me a cup of tea to revive me and then asked me to go out to the greenhouse and dig peonies for Della, he wasn't very strong, poor thing. At least she gave me some rubber boots."

"Ben, if she's giving Della her peonies, she thinks she's going to die."

Because she had decided not to sell the place, and instead of closing up entirely, she had closed her enterprise up bit by bit, as if she were a lizard shedding pieces of her tail, so that now only the very front of the greenhouse was operative, a wide space with a few favourite plants that could be watered by a spray system connected to her kitchen tap on days when she was bedridden. These included two blue tree peonies, treasures presented years ago by a grower who went to China for them, which Della had been trying to extract from her for years. Although she was fond of him—she called my "my dragonfly"—she had rapped his fingers for hinting and called him a bad boy. "When I'm dead," she always said.

Della Robbia: gorgeous pale pink, green at the heart, shading to violet at petals' edge. White veins and stamens, green anthers. Loose, floating form, luxuriant bloom, exotic for a Canadian hererocallis.

On Saturday she seemed very feeble, but she was funny
about Ben. "You should have seen him staring at Della,"
she chuckled. "And Della was in one of his moods, I
couldn't suppress him."

"You didn't want to," I said severely. "You're proud of
Della's eccentricities, if that's what you call them."

"Well, when you consider what he came from, and that
Dennis must be rolling in his grave."

Cordell was the strange fruit of Dennis' eldest son
Oliver, who had raised him on dirt farms and in men's
hostels until the rest of the Terryberries had taken a hand
to rescue him and sent him to a strict Anglican boarding-
school that taught mostly Latin and canoeing. "I'm worried; you gave him your peonies."

"You're jealous."

"You know I've no hand for tree peonies. You said he
couldn't have them until you died."

"He's designing for a textile competition, he'll need
them."

"I'm glad you've a reason. Do that exercise once more.
I can't feel the muscle." I had slid my hand under a but-
tock that was mere skin and bone; she pulled knee and
butt, but the muscle had no strength. "You'll have to try
harder, darling."

"You could let an old woman off."

"Have a rest, now, while I bring you your tea. If you
get just a little strength there your balance will improve."

"It's not balance I need, it's ballast." The more she ate,
the thinner she got, now.

"You don't look so good yourself," she said. "That Ben
wears you out."

I smiled, because on the Friday night he had, a little,
in a pleasant way. "You wore him out, Iris. He was scared

of Della."

"Those dratted he-men are sure it's catching."

"Well, Della's a slap in the face for them. He was impressed by the drawings."

"He's going into dark territory, that boy." I had a vision of Della at the mouth of Hades, blue torch of peony in his hands. Was it joy or terror on his face? "Let's try the exercise again, Iris."

The Herbaceous Peony Cerebrus: a deep maroon with golden stamens, shaggy and rich in form, was perhaps Miss Terryberry's most luxurious contribution to the Canadian garden, though the Terry series of iris cannot be faulted for purity of colour and richness of bloom, and she had a pleasant taste in daylilies. Her output was small—she refused to expand although there were several opportunities—and the select varieties she chose to work with responded almost lovingly to her touch. Whether you went to her for luscious Ellen Terry peonies, Terrylime and -lemon iris, or a basket of pansies and pinks, you felt privileged to be a customer. The old order changeth, there will not be another like her—Canadian Plant Breeders' Journal.

I was late getting out there the morning of her ninetieth birthday. Ronnie had made a fuss about getting into the car, and the coffee urn wasn't ready when I was passing the church to pick it up. She was sitting up in bed, neatly combed, wearing a pink silk jacket printed with mauve flowers that Della had sent her. She had died in her sleep. Ben came out with the doctor and Wilt's grandson Neil. They took both her and Ronnie away, and I stayed behind to wander the greenhouses and collect odd plants for the guests as she had wanted me to do. When Ben came back he dug up a row of firefly lilies she had promised me and that was that.

Or almost that. On the morning of the funeral I had an

appointment with Dr. Carscadden and asked him sharply what he had really thought of Iris. "Oh, I liked her," he said. "The one I had trouble with was Ardeen. She had the worst case of VD I'd ever seen, and I had a hard time coming to terms with that. I always do."

The funeral was God's own gift to Terryberry-watchers, the whole tribe led by Wilton (now 94 and victorious as the Oldest Surviving T) and Ronnie, who walked with downcast gaze, remote as an alcoholic from what was really going on, but sharp, I thought, in his child's way. Thence down through the generations to children with dark, sharp eyes and mischievous grins, and Della smart in a brass, buttoned blazer. Every florist in Western Ontario sent a wreath.

There was trouble afterwards when Wilton found out that Iris had sold her land to Ben years ago; he made a number of nasty remarks about Jews until Ben's lawyer pointed out that the amount of money that had changed hands was unnecessarily large.

Our wandering Aaron came home from British Columbia and lived out there for a while with his friend Blakey. Aaron hated the work, but Blakey took to it: he has green fingers. When I miss Iris, I go out there and help the boy. It's superbly boring work, but Blakey says, when he starts breeding I may name the flowers.

Louisa's Favourite: a lean brown day-lily, meagre-blooming, unruffled, but with golden stamens and strange, silver veins. Dignified, but merry in the breeze; unpredictable: not like anything else you have ever seen.

EDNA ALFORD divides her time between Alberta and Saskatchewan. She is the author of two collections of stories, *A Sleep Full of Dreams* and *The Garden of Eloise Loon*.

SHELDON CURRIE teaches at St. Francis Xavier University. He has appeared in many periodicals, has published a collection of stories called *The Glace Bay Miner's Museum* and is currently finishing a novel called *A Supermarket in Glace Bay*.

MARIAN ENGEL's posthumous collection of stories, *The Tattooed Woman*, was recently released by Penguin Books.

DOUGLAS GLOVER won the *Canadian Fiction Magazine* contributor's prize for the story that appears in this collection. His first book, *The Mad River*, was published in 1981. His first novel, *Precious*, appeared in 1984. He lives in Waterford, Ontario.

MARION JOHNSON is of Icelandic-Canadian background. She has a PhD in linguistics and has worked in the Northwest Territories as a language researcher. She lives in London, Ontario. "Coming of Age in Canada" is the first fiction she has published.

W.P. KINSELLA is best known as the author of *Dance Me Outside*. His later books about Silas Ermineskin include *Scars, Born Indian* and *The Moccasin Telegraph*, and his novel *Shoeless Joe* won a Houghton Mifflin Literary Fellowship.

NORMAN LEVINE's most recent book is a collection entitled *Champagne Barn* published in the Penguin Short Fiction series. This story was written, on a commission by

Robert Weaver, for the 30th anniversary of the CBC radio program *Anthology*.

JOYCE MARSHALL was born in Montreal but currently lives in Toronto. She is the author of two novels and a collection of short stories, and has appeared in a great many story anthologies, most recently, *Illuminations, The Anthology Anthology* and *Stories by Canadian Women*.

JANE RULE lives on Galiano Island. She has published a number of novels, short-story collections and essays. Forthcoming are a collection of stories and another collection of prose pieces that explores the borderlines of story, essay and autobiography.

ROBERT G. SHERRIN was born in Ottawa but now lives in Vancouver. He has published one novel, *The Black Box*, and is currently working on another, as well as more short stories.

CAROL WINDLEY was born in Tofino, on the west coast of Vancouver Island and currently lives in Nanaimo. She has published poetry, but "Moths," which appeared in *Event*, was her first publication of a work of fiction.

Acknowledgements: "At Mrs. Warder's House" by Edna
Alford first appeared in *Descant,* as did "Man in the Black
Magic Box" by Robert G. Sherrin. "The Accident" by
Sheldon Currie and "Dog Attempts to Drown Man in
Saskatoon" by Douglas Glover first appeared in *Canadian
Fiction Magazine.* "Django, Karfunkelstein & Roses" by
Norman Levine appeared in *Canadian Forum.* "Avis de
Vente" by Joyce Marshall first appeared in *Matrix* and
"Under the Hill" by Marian Engel is taken from *The
Tattooed Woman,* copyright © the Estate of Marian Engel
and reprinted by permission of Penguin Books Canada
Ltd.

ISBN 0 88750 589 9 (hardcover)
ISBN 0 88750 590 2 (softcover)
ISSN 0703 9476

Cover photograph by Greg Stott
Book design by Michael Macklem

Printed in Canada

PUBLISHED IN CANADA BY OBERON PRESS